SIMON & SCHUSTER CHILDREN'S PUBLISHING
ADVANCE READER'S COPY

TITLE: The Danger of Small Things

AUTHOR: Caryl Lewis

IMPRINT: Atheneum

ON-SALE DATE: 3/24/26

ISBN: 978-1-6659-7751-7

FORMAT: hardcover

PRICE: $19.99 / $27.99 CAN

AGES: 12 up

PAGES: 272

Do not quote for publication until verified with finished books. This advance uncorrected reader's proof is the property of Simon & Schuster. It is being loaned for promotional purposes and review by the recipient and may not be used for any other purpose or transferred to any third party. Simon & Schuster reserves the right to cancel the loan and recall possession of the proof at any time. Any duplication, sale, or distribution to the public is a violation of law.

Please send any review or mention of this book to
ChildrensPublicity@simonandschuster.com.

Aladdin · Atheneum Books for Young Readers
Beach Lane Books · Beyond Words · Boynton Bookworks
Caitlyn Dlouhy Books · Denene Millner Books
Libros para niños · Little Simon · Margaret K. McElderry Books
MTV Books · Paula Wiseman Books · Salaam Reads
Sarah Barley Books · Simon & Schuster Books for Young Readers
Simon Pulse · Simon Spotlight

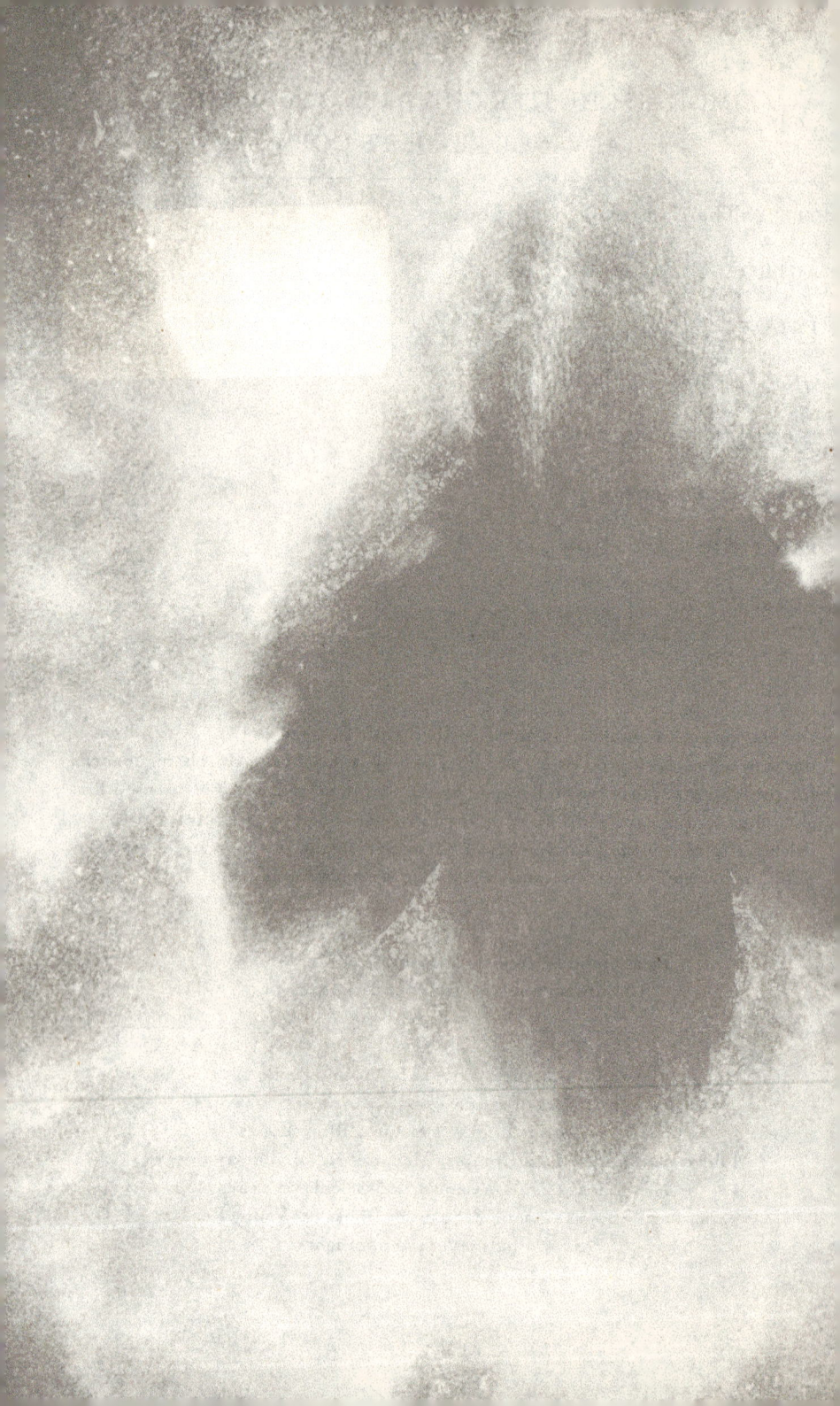

the danger of small things

caryl lewis

NEW YORK · AMSTERDAM/ANTWERP
LONDON · TORONTO
SYDNEY/MELBOURNE · NEW DELHI

An imprint of Simon & Schuster Children's Publishing Division
1230 Avenue of the Americas, New York, New York 10020
For more than 100 years, Simon & Schuster has championed authors and the stories they create.
By respecting the copyright of an author's intellectual property, you enable Simon & Schuster
and the author to continue publishing exceptional books for years to come. We thank you for
supporting the author's copyright by purchasing an authorized edition of this book.
No amount of this book may be reproduced or stored in any format, nor may it be uploaded to any
website, database, language-learning model, or other repository, retrieval, or artificial intelligence
system without express permission. All rights reserved. Inquiries may be directed to Simon & Schuster,
1230 Avenue of the Americas, New York, NY 10020 or permissions@simonandschuster.com.
This book is a work of fiction. Any references to historical events, real people, or real places are used
fictitiously. Other names, characters, places, and events are products of the author's imagination, and
any resemblance to actual events or places or persons, living or dead, is entirely coincidental.
Text © 2026 by Caryl Lewis
Jacket photograph of dust by Avesun/iStock
Jacket illustration of bee by Oksana Kovaleva/iStock
All rights reserved, including the right of reproduction in whole or in part in any form.
Atheneum logo is a trademark of Simon & Schuster, LLC.
For information about special discounts for bulk purchases, please contact Simon & Schuster
Special Sales at 1-866-506-1949 or business@simonandschuster.com.
Simon & Schuster strongly believes in freedom of expression and stands against
censorship in all its forms. For more information, visit BooksBelong.com.
The Simon & Schuster Speakers Bureau can bring authors to your live event. For more
information or to book an event, contact the Simon & Schuster Speakers Bureau at
1-866-248-3049 or visit our website at www.simonspeakers.com.
The text for this book was set in Mrs Eaves.
Manufactured in the United States of America
First Edition
2 4 6 8 10 9 7 5 3 1
CIP data for this book is available from the Library of Congress.
ISBN 9781665977517
ISBN 9781665977531 (ebook)

For Gwenno, who inspired this book.
Paint. Dance. Light the match.

Imagination is the only weapon
in the war against reality.

—Unknown

1.

The world ended years before anyone realized it had, in complete silence. I can't stop thinking about it, about when and where it might've happened; whether it happened in the folds of a flower in someone's back garden, or in a concrete carpark, or at the side of a city street on a gray morning as people bustled past, heads down to catch their train? No one was listening, but that day a hum left the world, a noise that no one had noticed was there until it was long gone, leaving behind a terrifying, sterile silence. And I still can't believe that no one frowned, no one turned their head and noticed the absence of something. The truth is that the whole world rested on a single bee's wings. The whole world. The mists over the greatest forests, old people walking hand in hand, countries, oceans, storms, languages, children, cities, freedoms, and dreams. Everything. Everything rested on those translucent wings. They were fragile as stained glass, and they carried the weight of the world—until we shattered them.

Cass says I'll get punished if they hear me talking about it. She always flicks her red plait over her shoulder, crosses her arms, and tells me that it cannot be undone, that you cannot piece a bee's wings back together again, so why do I torture myself? And I try not to, it's just that every night after everyone falls into bed exhausted, I wake up a few hours later, my body taut and strung out on this thin mattress. I look up at the bottom of Cass's bunk—at the slats that look like train tracks—and these thoughts just will not stop coming and coming and my breathing gets all shallow like I can't get enough oxygen out of the air and all I can think about is how those broken wings collapsed a hive and how in that moment the balance of the universe tipped.

I listen as Cass turns over in her bunk, tune in to her breathing, and try to match my breaths to hers. Breathe in, breathe out, swallow down the panic. I look at the strand of hair that's falling in a curve off the side of her bed, set free from the day's tight plaits. Although I can't see her face, I know her skin is damp from sweat, her freckled cheeks sunburned under her eyes, the fan on the ceiling seemingly just moving heat around the bunkhouse. And for a moment, I can almost imagine that we are safe. It's just a bunk, a striped mattress, and a lock of Cass's hair in the darkness.

They said it was frightening how quickly it happened. News banners scrolling across screens saying that crops were failing and experts talking about it, their faces tense, explaining how only crops pollinated by wind would survive. Before long, certain foods became scarce, and within decades, you couldn't really go outside in summer and the rains just would not come. And then in desperation, people plundered the sea for food, and the wars started and the famines, and the borders closed, and communications broke down, and everything fell to pieces. Eventually everyone was given identity papers, girls weren't allowed outside anymore, and boys had to learn to fight.

Mum hid us as long as she could, longer than she should have. Every Monday morning she'd go to the ration line in the city center. Shey would wrap his arms around her and tell her to be careful out there and then I'd go and distract myself by sitting by the window, studying the sky as it moved from watery blue to a sickly sallow color as the day exhausted itself. She'd gotten someone she knew to fudge our dates of birth on the documents and she had to stand in line for hours, a knife in the back waistband of her old jeans in case she ran into trouble. When she got home, we'd share whatever she'd been able to get. Bread, usually, and pasta; there hadn't been milk or meat for months. Shey was growing so fast, and Mum would stop eating halfway through her food, saying she wasn't hungry anymore, and would push her plate toward Shey even though I could see that she was swallowing her own spit, trying to trick her brain into thinking that she was full.

I'd ask her what it was like before the collapse, but she said she didn't remember, only what her parents told her, and I'd make her tell me those stories over and over so I could kind of push out the edges of the world, and when we were old enough, she taught us to read, like her parents had taught her. You had to hide books or they'd be taken away and burned by the militia—they were trying to stop people from thinking too much. We must have read the ones hidden in the house a thousand times before Ruth next door gave us some more. Ruth was really old, much too old to work, so they'd cut back her rations to the minimum, and she was on her own. Mum would help her out, and in return she got these books.

The best one was an encyclopedia. Mum ripped the pages out of it and pasted them all around the inside walls of the house. Pictures of oceans and forests and these animals that I just couldn't imagine used to be real. These things called chameleons that could change color and these blue butterflies that could cross the whole earth. And sometimes by flashlight, she'd make shadows on the walls with her hands and tell us stories of hummingbirds, which had iridescent green wings, and these things called coral reefs, which were teeming with fish of every size and color, and these wavy, frondy underwater forests. We'd lie on the bed, all three of us, looking up at the pictures in the dark, and sometimes she'd be trying to tell us something about how angry she was when the camps were set up and the military took over and she'd just cry, and Shey would get upset and look away, and I'd wrap my arms around her middle, and I could feel her mood shift from this warm marigold orange to this emptied-out muddy green.

Most girls were brought here at eleven. I got thirteen years with Mum and Shey. That's more than anyone else in this place got. Seven hundred and thirty days more, to be precise.

I remember asking her, though. Mum. Why. Why didn't they do anything? Before that last bee died, before the seasons changed, and she'd just shrug. Say that perhaps people thought that the world would end in a cacophony. That something momentous would happen like the moon becoming untethered from Earth, or a bomb dropping, filling the world with screaming. I suppose they couldn't see the danger in small things. They thought that whispers could be ignored. They couldn't see that a thread could unravel a tapestry, or that a single bee could destroy the world.

2.

"Jess, wake up."

Cass's voice sounds far away even as I feel her close. She shakes my shoulders, pulls on my arm. She's standing at our bunk in bare feet and a vest, and I squint at her as she pulls her hair over her shoulder like a curtain and rakes her fingers through it.

"The bell's going to go," she says, frowning. I groan.

"Come on, don't be grumpy."

I try to bring her into focus, haul myself up to sitting, my body feeling heavy. I sit a moment, watch her tug at her hair, then she turns her back to me and parks herself on the floor between my legs, her back against the hard edge of the bunk, and without talking I start plaiting her hair. Every morning begins like this, separating out the parts of her hair and trying not to get my fingers in a knot as I do my best to remember the pattern she likes, over then under, under then over.

The whole dorm is almost silent at this time in the morning, save for the sharp intake of breath if someone's hair snags or begins to tangle at the ends and is pulled too harshly. There are no rules as such on how to plait it, just that it's tight and out of the way for work, but the patterns get more and more elaborate as some of the girls compete with one another. Depending on the texture of their hair, there are braids and Dutch plaits and French plaits, styles from different cultures, and I am getting better at it. Some of the girls had sisters, so theirs are usually tidier. Cass tips her head forward to make it easier for me as I get to the bottom of the plait and tie it off with string.

I touch her shoulders like I do every morning to signal that I've finished, and even though she knows she has to get up and I know I have to get up, we sit a moment, and I think that it is the best time of day. Just the quiet, and the cooler air of morning before work begins, Cass and me sitting in silence, her white legs out in front of her, her palms laid flat on her thighs.

The bell rings. Crassly. Jarringly. Making my stomach turn over like it does every morning, and then the buzzing of the radio loudspeaker cranks up with recorded messages from the militia. Be dutiful. Work hard. We're in this together. I get up, tuck my short hair behind my ears, reach for my washrag, and walk to the end of the dorm. There are around fifty bunks in here, a hundred girls in each of the five buildings, and even after months of being here, I still can't quite get used to the sheer number of people, the relentlessness of the chatter. The ceilings are low, the buildings narrow and suffocating. The walls are bare except for a few solar lights and there are three chairs for the Mothers to sit on to keep an eye on us. Not that they are mothers;

they work for the camp, have been through the system, know every trick in the book. They come in as we stand in line, waiting to wash, and take their places.

Mother Clement keeps watch in our section, and I don't understand how her presence feels so heavy for such a small woman. If she were a color, she'd be a sludgy gray, thick and pallid. As she goes to sit, she clasps her short fingers and tucks her crossed legs underneath the seat neatly. I don't know what I thought when I arrived here, perhaps there was a part of me that thought they might accidentally care a little—that the word "Mother" might mean something. But the truth is that they have this unshakable indifference, Mother Clement in particular. There's nothing in her face at all, no emotion, no expression, and she reports anyone who steps out of line with this casual, brutal efficiency. The first time she saw me, she took in my short hair, resolved to dislike me, and for weeks whenever I'd look up, she'd be watching me. I hold my rag against my chest, stand behind Cass, and lean my forehead on the back of her shoulder before noticing how her shoulder blades are jutting out. I lift my head and look at her back. The bones of her spine, her neck in a knotted line. She's looking thinner, and for some reason, I feel like I should look away.

Ruth said that there were towels when she was a kid, white cotton ones that would envelop you, but cotton disappeared a long time ago. It was strange, she said, the things you missed. She missed her first and only proper job when she was a young girl. She went to study nursing, worked in the community; she said she used to chat with people, drink tea, and she even missed the rain, well, normal rain, not the deluges that happened now that sweep all the soil away.

She missed these things called plays too. On the weekends, she'd go to these places called theaters, where they used to act things out. That was people's job, she said, making up stories and acting them out for other people, and sometimes, I'd sit on the floor and she'd tell me about all the shows that she'd seen. She showed me a map once too, one she'd had since she was a kid. She'd rubbed some countries out—colored them in red—but you could see where they'd been. She said that Tuvalu, the Solomon Islands, and Kiribati disappeared first, once the sea levels rose. Then the hottest countries became unbearable to live in. There were millions of refugees and not enough food.

I try to tune out the banging in the Food Hall as breakfast is put out on trays next door. There's a rhythm to every day: we get up, we tie our hair back, we wash, we eat, we work, we eat, we are given a few hours to rest outside before washing once again and sleeping. Cass and I step forward every now and again as each girl disappears behind a screen, tugs off her vest and pants, and washes under her armpits and between her legs, rubs herself dry. The floors are wet and stink in the heat. I watch as Cass disappears behind the screen.

"You're never gonna wash yourself clean," a familiar voice whispers in my ear. I know who it is. I don't turn around but I feel my face hardening. Like this mask comes over my eyes and my mouth and my features just kind of freeze.

"Traitor," she whispers.

I wait as Cass washes and wonder whether I should turn around. I notice that the room has quieted a little, the low-grade chatting turned down a level as the others sense something going on. Mother Clement doesn't take notice. Charmian has coarse brown hair to her waist, olive skin that doesn't burn. The prettier you are, the more powerful you are and the more the Mothers will look away and let us get on with it. It's strange, but when Charmian walks into a room, you can feel her before you see her, like a draft.

"Scum."

Charmian's breath is on my ear now. Pins and needles of dread make their way up my neck until they congregate on my burning cheeks. I catch Mother Clement's eye, and she turns away. The stupid thing is I know what I'd do if this were Shey. If it were Shey, I'd turn around and punch him. I'd slap him hard, and he'd probably hit me back and we'd fight like that until Mum would lay her palm on her forehead and ask what the hell we were doing, but then we'd be best friends and it would all be over, but this? Here? This is different. There are no fair fights, just a group of girls locked up together because of our age, suspicion everywhere. They'd stared at me when I arrived, my short hair so different from theirs, they'd laugh when I walked past, whispers all around. Thank goodness for Cass.

"Scum," Charmian whispers again, and just as she does, Cass comes out from behind the screen and takes in the scene. Her face darkens.

"It's your turn," she says to me slowly while locking eyes with Charmian to let her know that she's watching her, and

I step forward, my stomach aching from tension and hunger and anger, and as I start to wash, I notice my hands are shaking and I'm suddenly angry, not at Charmian but at my hands, at my stupid, damn hands.

I'm not hungry anymore, so I wait for Cass at the truck. I can see her scanning the crowd for me and I look up to catch her eyes. She comes to stand next to me, her long skirt dragging in the dust, her straw hat casting a shadow on the bottom half of her face. She looks at me and I just shrug, not wanting to think about Charmian anymore. There are twenty trucks—each carrying twenty-five girls—and they start their engines one after the other. The guards start shouting and the red dust starts to roll across the camp.

"We'd better get on," Cass says, and I follow her, the dryness starting to bite at my throat.

The first time I saw the camp, I couldn't take it in. The scale of it. I stood in the back of the khaki truck, pressed up against everyone else as we traveled across its length. The five interconnected bunkhouses in a semicircle, each with its own washing area, ringed with an enclosed exercise yard. Beyond that the Mothers' Quarters and the headquarters, around which stood a gray concrete wall. There were only two exit points, one to the road to the city and the one we used most days—the road to the crops.

That first day I watched as the girls covered their mouths with their sleeves, held their hats on their heads so they wouldn't blow away. Through the undulating heat I saw the perimeter wall come into view. The top of it bristling with barbs, soldiers walking its length, their guns casually slung on their shoulders. It wasn't the sound of those massive electric gates opening, blowing up more red dust, that was most terrifying, it was the fact that the soldiers jeered, shouted. They bayed like dogs, something in their eyes making me feel really small, and I remember pushing my way into the middle of the girls so I didn't have to see their faces as we passed. After that the gates closed once again, and we drove for a long time. A couple of hours or more, the heat beating down on us, and I kept my head down, tried to shut out the talking girls, until the truck abruptly stopped, and a soldier clanged the side of it with the butt of his gun. I didn't know what was happening, but I felt more room around me and I was carried in the crowd toward the steps at the back of the truck. I tried not to trip as I was pushed down the stairs. And then I lifted my head.

It was like my eyes couldn't process it at first. Or perhaps my eyes could, but my mind couldn't make sense of it. There were rows of trees as far as I could see. As far as the horizon, trees planted in straight lines, and a vast watering system in action because the soil was so dry. Through the haze of the heat, I saw hundreds of girls on ladders, each one brushing, brushing the blossoms. Pollinating the flowers. It was like someone had stolen my breath. And I remember standing, trying to take it in, the strangeness of it, the awesome scale of it, until the girl behind me shoved the back of my shoulder, and I followed the girls in front of me by walking down the row of trees we were supposed to work on, two girls shearing off at each tree until it was our turn. The girl I was paired with fetched one of the ladders that had been left on the ground for us to use.

"Wake up, you idiot," she spat through these gritted teeth. "Get one yourself, then."

And I did what she said, I picked up a ladder, wrangled it, and walked to lay it against the trunk of the tree we were working on. Then I climbed up it. My hands were shaking, the apple blossoms all around me, and I took the brush out of my apron pocket where it had to be always kept and copied the girl I was working with. I began to pollinate the blossoms, by hand. Moving the golden powder from one flower to another, again and again and again until my arm ached.

Cass leans her head on my shoulder as we head south. It's probably apple trees today again. Sometimes it's cherry, sometimes peaches. I don't know where the fruit goes. I think it's to trade with other countries for arms, for food and provisions. Cass says you have to tune out the noise of everything, but I can't. Not really. I've tried to tune out the soldiers at the perimeters, the chatter of the other girls, the routine of it all, but you can't, not if you are capable of imagining something that's not this.

The truck stops and I wake Cass, who's fallen asleep on my shoulder. The girls start filing off two by two. I step in behind Cass so that we can work together. We drop down the steps and start walking along the line of trees. Cass stops and grabs a ladder; I do the same as we have done over and over again.

I don't know when I realized, it can't have been very long

after that first day. It's funny now, when I think back, but I remember thinking that there was something peaceful about it, being here, in that fragrance, in these white flowers. That if this was what I'd have to do, it wasn't so bad, and then I turned my head and looked down the line of trees that stretched farther than I could see and I understood that this was to be my life until I myself could bear fruit, have a baby, and that my life and my body were no longer my own.

3.

The soil gets everywhere. In your eyes, in your hair, in your lungs. It clings to you even after you wash it away. Sometimes it feels as if we are just in the process of turning to dust. Cass has already washed, let down her hair, and is wearing her Second Dress. She's lying barefoot on her bunk quietly. I pull my Second Dress over my head, feeling the heaviness of Cass's silence around me. All the dresses are the same, floor length, high collar, long sleeves. Nothing that will show our bodies; it's to keep us safe, they say. The First Dresses are work ones and are a brown check, and the Second Dresses are gray, both a kind of nylon material. Every one of them has a patch of stray threads on the breast patch where name labels have been sewn on and taken off and sewn on again as girls come and go.

"We'd better hurry up," I say, and watch as Cass lies still for a little longer. I reluctantly reach out and touch her arm, and eventually she swings her legs off the side of the bunk.

The Assembly Hall is the biggest room in the camp, and we're taken there every two weeks for the latest report on the brushing and for the ceremonies. There's a concrete floor, bars on the windows, a kind of stage, and on the wall to the left a portrait of General Porter, his bronzed face pouting petulantly. Ruth used to say that they had these Assemblies when she was in school with praying and stuff and music, but there's none of that now. Schools closed before Mum was born. We find the girls our age and line up with them. The younger girls eat earlier than us, are in different dorms, are trucked out to brush together. This is one of the only times we see them. They stand in line in front, and the girls get gradually taller as you get to the back of the hall. Once all five hundred girls are in the hall, it never feels like there's enough air to go around. The guards all take their places at the entrances. I look around. There's no one here above sixteen.

Then there's clapping as Father Renatus comes to the stage. I feel myself recoil at the sight of him, get this feeling in the pit of my stomach. The thing about him is that he doesn't look like the kind of man who would run a camp like this. He's pretty young, doesn't look much older than thirty-five, he's slight, his skin waxy. Sometimes the new girls blush at the sight of him, but to me he looks like the kind of man who looks for power in the softest places.

As always, we have to pledge our allegiance to the general, hand on hearts, and as usual I find myself moving my mouth, not saying the words although I know them by heart. "I pledge my life to serving our community." I try to block out the girls whispering all around and have learned not to even make the effort to mouth the words properly in case they get the chance to embed themselves further in my brain. "I give my labor, my body, and my life, and will demonstrate unconditional obedience to General Porter for as long as I live." I feel a wash of relief when the hall falls silent again.

"I'm glad to report that we're making good progress in all the zones. The percentage of fruit set after pollination is within the expected levels. We'll keep an eye on this in the next couple of weeks and adjust your distribution as necessary, so thank you for your hard work."

He throws away the last part of the sentence, the modulation in his voice revealing it to be habit rather than sentiment and that he's already thinking about his next task. He looks down at the little girls.

"So, after the formalities, our first job today is to welcome all our new girls."

There's vague clapping, mostly by those standing closest to the guards.

"I'm sure you'll be very happy here and will do your best to be good girls."

I can feel myself wincing and Cass digs her elbow into my ribs.

"You must do your duty now and work hard. Brushing is a very important role. It is vital we keep the crops pollinated so we can feed our communities, keeping them healthy and ready for the future. I need not remind you that we are a team in this camp, doing our best for our city in a very hostile world. Mistakes were made in the past, profit was put before people, injustice was rife, those with money and influence were corrupted and the earth paid the price, indeed we all paid a price. As we learn from the mistakes of the past, we'll build a new world together, putting people first, prioritizing equality and fairness. We all have to make sacrifices now, you, the Mothers who care for you, and of course me myself. We do this for one another, we do this as a family."

I find myself digging my nails into the palms of my hands, his words as cloying now as they were the first time I heard them.

Then he turns and nods at the Mother who's waiting at the side of the stage. At this I feel Cass stiffen as around seventeen young women walk onto the stage. They're all dressed the same, but this time they have special blue-colored dresses on that are deeper than the tone of the sky and have a hint of green about them, and their hair is tied back loosely in ponytails. But even though they're dressed the same, the sameness can't cancel their differences. Some have their shoulders stooped and are obviously terrified. Some are enjoying their moment in the limelight, and some seem defiant.

"Can we give them a round of applause, please?"

There come some clapping and a few shouts, some of the girls shifting their weight from one leg to the other, and then the chair is produced.

"All these girls are now women; husbands have been chosen for them based on their fertility compatibility, and they are now legally married. Let's congratulate them as they move on to do their duty as wives and mothers."

There's less noise now as one of the girls is marched to the chair and pressure is put on her shoulders to make her sit. I know what's coming, I've seen it so many times before, but it's still as shocking each time. The nonchalance of the Mothers, the tense hush in the room. We watch as the girl's eyes run everywhere and then one of the Mothers goes to stand behind her, takes some scissors out of her apron, winds the girl's long hair into a tight coil, and starts to hack it off. The girl covers her face with her hands, her head yanked this way and that as the job is hurriedly done. The Mother then throws the hair into a basket beside the chair and pushes the girl to her feet, beckoning the next one. At this, the girl stands shaken, exposed on the stage, looking back at her hair. Feeling the different weight on her now.

Cass is older than me by almost a year and knows it won't be long for her, that it cannot be long for her as she's almost fourteen. That's why she's always quiet before Assembly. Ruth said that girls used to start their periods much earlier when she was young, before people couldn't get enough to eat. It's almost as if our bodies are reluctant to bring children into this world. Cass will probably start soon, and if she doesn't, then that is equally as bad. Women who can't have babies are pushed out, or worse; after all, they're a useless mouth to feed.

We watch as girl after girl has their hair butchered, held up as something the youngest girls in the front should aspire to, and I can feel myself sicken. The heat, and the sound of the scissors cutting through the lengths of their hair. The way the Mother scowls when a young girl with beautiful, tight curly hair sits down, her expressions as she hacks at it, the way she throws it into a different basket. I see a girl in the row in front shift her weight at this, the way she pushes out her chin. My stomach turns, and then, thankfully, it is over.

I hold on to Cass as we file out of the hall, the new

graduates taken away. Some of them are crying. They will be "free" to leave when their new husbands come to collect them, given extra ration vouchers when they are pregnant, encouraged to have large families in order to help out the community. At last, we file through the door, and I follow Cass out into the exercise yard where we'll be allowed to stay until bedtime, and we make our way toward the perimeter fence where we usually sit. We're almost there when Cass grabs my hand. She looks at me.

"Cass? What's wrong?"

"I can't breathe," she says. She's pale, her hands trembling. She looks terrified.

"What do you mean?"

"I can't breathe," she says.

I hold her hands, lock eyes with her. "It's okay."

She's shaking her head.

"You're panicking, try to breathe."

"I can't see, everything's blurry," she gasps. There are tears on her face now.

"Just slowly breathe. . . ."

"I don't know what's happening." She puts out her hand, crumples to her knees, and I kneel down with her, press my chest to hers.

"Breathe when I breathe, only when I breathe." I feel her trying to match my breaths, in and out, in and out, for about a minute until her shoulders start to become less tense. She sinks down a little, and I put my arm around her.

"Can you see?"

She nods through the tears.

"I need to know they're looking after us—they are, aren't they?" she asks breathlessly.

Some girls come up to us to supposedly help, but more to see what's going on, so I wave them away with my arm and a scowl. I listen to Cass breathe.

"Jess?" she asks again.

I wish I could answer her. When I first arrived, I was shocked by her trust, by her faith, by her belief in the system, and sometimes it was like she could sense my skepticism and would press me about it. Like she wanted to know more but didn't want to hear it either. It was like she was picking at a scab, guessing all the while what I really thought and that my answer would sting.

"It's okay, just breathe," I whisper, trying to distract her.

"I wish there was somewhere else we could go," Cass says.

I wait for her breathing to settle, and eventually she drops her head into my lap, exhausted, and we sit for a long time. I look over at the fence and the tall wall beyond that encircles the camp. The shadows are lengthening, the patterns of the mesh and netting falling across the dry earth, and in the distance I hear the faint buzz of the loudspeaker cars that circle the city broadcasting yet another overnight lockdown. Making sure everyone is inside.

"You know I once read a book where a young boy found another world through the back of a wardrobe," I say quietly. "There was a snow queen there."

Cass is quiet for a moment.

"And a lion, a beautiful lion with a huge mane."

"I don't know why your mum bothered to teach you to

read," Cass murmurs. "It's such made-up stuff. But I am kind of glad that she did."

I smile, stroke her head. It's getting darker now, the sky turning a dangerous blue red. It's cooler too as some of the girls start heading to bed, their figures looking black in the distance.

"Can you imagine snow? Being that cold?" I say softly.

I know we're both trying to imagine it now in the silence. I tease a knot from one of the strands of her hair with my fingers.

"What . . . what else did you read?" she asks quietly. Her nose still sounding blocked. The skin on her face blotchy.

"There was one about a secret garden by this huge house. A robin, it was a type of bird, brown with this really bright-red belly . . ."

Cass laughs softly now. "That can't be real. . . . ," she says in disbelief.

"Yes, it was, there were robins, with these red bellies, and this one helps this little girl find the key to a door, and through the door, there's the most beautiful secret garden in the world. And there are birds and trees and shelter and shade and everything's green and lush and magical."

Cass's eyes are far away now.

I shrug. "Maybe there's one here and we just don't know it."

She's smiling now as the bell begins to ring. I know she doesn't want to move, I don't either. We sit there for as long as we can, waiting until everyone else has made their way in before I pull her to her feet, let her lean on me. We walk back to the bunkhouse, both of us thinking what other worlds there could be.

4.

Cass's eyes are still swollen from crying. She must've looked tired, because Deva gave her more breakfast than usual this morning, slid some extra bread on her tray. I watched her eat, but I could tell she wasn't hungry. I pushed her vitamins toward her, the synthetic ones they give us to make up for the fact that we can't get everything we need from the food anymore.

We get on the truck, and for the first time in a while, there are free seats, so I pull her hand toward me, and we sit. Cass is already leaning her head on the bars of the truck, her eyes closed as we set off.

We're going north today, and I've always preferred to be on this side. There's no real difference of course; the landscape is as barren as it is anywhere, the heat just as harsh. It's just that I feel closer to freedom here somehow. There's another city a few hundred miles away, but beyond that, no one knows. Mum said she'd heard rumors that if you keep heading north as far as you can, that the land there has fared better, it being so cold to start with, and that some species survived there, are *still* surviving there.

My hand goes to my lap and my apron, the brush as always in the pocket, and I let my mind go to Ruth and the stories she told me of how her father kept bees. When she was little, she said that she would follow him every day begging for him to explain things until he gave in and started to teach her. And she'd paint these pictures with words: the late summer sun, gentle not harsh, and the smell of the hive as you opened it. When I was small, I would draw bees and she'd make me do it again and again until they looked just right.

I never really thought about it, not until I started brushing, but Ruth said that bees would visit up to five thousand flowers a day, five *thousand*. A hive would pollinate millions of flowers over a summer. I've thought about it a lot since starting. At first my arms ached so much, my left from grabbing the ladder all day and my right from holding the brush up. At night they'd be numb with pins and needles, and I'd wake up not being able to move them. I can feel my arms getting stronger, my fingers more used to holding the brush. My balance is better too, and the front of my knees don't ache so much from leaning my weight on a ladder rung, but we're so stupidly slow. We're so stupidly slow even when we're working as fast as we can. The blossoms flower for such a short time, and the rows of trees are never-ending. I don't know what we're meant for, but it's not this. We're too big, the gnarly branches nick our faces, tip the hats from our heads. Yes, our brushes do the job, but clumsily.

Ruth said that even after all that work, the bees would only make a quarter spoonful of honey in their whole lives. I asked her to describe the taste of it to me once and she laughed, ruffled my hair, and said it was like your tongue being stung with sweetness, bitterness, with storms and sadness. She said it tasted like a longing for life, like the bees longed for the flowers, which were outside of themselves. I tried to imagine it in the only way I knew how, by painting a picture of her, of flowers blooming in her mouth, and she pinned it to her bedroom wall. Then she showed me a picture of a bee in a flower, its body covered in gold dust, and how it savored the nectar. The thing was, though, that the bee got something back. It was rewarded for its work. It was a relationship of giving and receiving. I don't know what we're getting.

We drive over a bump, which knocks Cass awake; she sits up, thinks we're there. I smile at her, and her panic dissipates, and she relaxes again. Looks out.

"It's smoky," she says quietly. There's a haze hanging in the air. Heavy.

I look across at the city. There have been more fires recently. More rioting, protests around rationing and water, the way soldiers beat people up over the smallest things. The smoke often rolls in waves across the camp and the sounds of sirens bleed into the night.

"Perhaps it's a good thing," I offer. "A sign people have had enough, that things will change." But Cass doesn't seem convinced.

Cass doesn't like to talk about it. Doesn't like to talk about anything beyond the now, and I understand. It's like she's fenced off areas too, and every time I talk about things beyond the camp limits, she shrinks a little. I don't even know why I keep bringing them up, but I can't let it go. It's like I get energy from it, the thought of a revolution makes me feel a little more alive.

"It's definitely getting worse," I say to Cass. "The smoke, it's almost every other day."

The sound of spiky laughter cuts across us and I feel the girls standing nearby rearranging themselves.

"We're gonna have some fun tonight. . . ." It's Charmian. "We're organizing a competition," she says.

I stare straight ahead. Cass doesn't know where to look.

Charmian studies my face, I can feel her eyes on me. "You two gonna take part? Come on . . . what do you say? Or are you gonna be spoilsports?" she needles us.

The truck driver brakes hard, and she is almost thrown onto me. I push her back and she laughs loudly.

"Oh sorry, I didn't see you there," she exclaims as the other girls laugh behind her.

Cass grabs my arm, a silent sign to just let Charmian get off the truck first. I stand, my jaw clenched as she pushes past.

"It's okay," says Cass quietly, and I really want to believe her.

✦ ✦ ✦ ✦

A wind has started up, which makes brushing harder. It disturbs the soil to start with and threatens to blow away the pollen, which makes the pollination patchier. Cass and I start work and we pull down our hats so that the brims are low over our eyes. I hate it when it's like this because we can't hear each other speak. We can't even see each other. When it's calm, we have a game where we catch glimpses of each other framed in flowers and leaves like portraits and we try to make the strangest faces. Today it's just heat and wind and dryness and it's getting into my eyes. I wonder how long they'll keep us out here in this.

There are no real seasons now. Brushing goes on most of the year, and when we're not outside, Cass says there are greenhouses. Miles and miles of them with artificial solar lights, and that's where we're taken for the other months of the year. It's taking so long today since the blossoms move about, making it difficult to get to the pollen, and as I look up, I see Cass stop for a moment. She looks scared; she's hanging on to the top rung of the ladder now with both hands.

"Cass?" My voice is carried away by the wind.

I look across at the nearest guard, his gun slung across his back. He's noticed too and is looking across. I wait a moment. "Cass?" I try again. "Cass?!"

She's stepping down the ladder now.

"Cass, what are you doing?"

She stumbles halfway down, her skirt catching in the heel of her shoe, and she slips, falling to the floor. My heart clenches and I drop my brush. I hurry down my ladder without thinking and around the trunk of the tree. I can see the guard coming nearer.

She's breathing funny again.

"Cass? Is it the same as last night?" I ask. I'm on my knees now, holding the sides of her arms.

She nods.

"Breathe with me, breathe with me, Cass. Block everything else out."

There's a shadow across us. "What's going on?"

He must be around seventeen, dark hair, his face tanned, his uniform dusty.

"She's fine," I say. Cass looks up at me without speaking.

"Does she need a medical?"

"NO!" Cass shouts, trying to get up.

"It's okay," I say to her, looking her in the eyes, trying to reassure her, then I turn to the guard. "She needs water, that's all."

The guard sits down on his heels, studies Cass for a moment. I feel his nearness, the tip of the gun almost touching my face. Then he reaches for his canteen of water and offers it to her. She looks at me and I nod. She drinks, breathes, drinks. Now he's closer, he looks younger still, not much older than Shey. A sewn-on badge with loose threads on his uniform. O'Brien. I look away, my jaw clenched.

"It's hard today, eh?" he says quietly.

I resist the urge to scream at him but can't stop myself laughing bitterly. He looks at me, seemingly genuinely hurt.

"Does she need to sit in the truck awhile?" he asks.

"No, she doesn't," I say. "She's fine." I start to pull her to her feet, and to my relief, she stands.

"She'd be safe there," he says. I push her behind me and round on him. "She's fine," I say, slightly louder than I'd anticipated. He nods, puts the lid back on the canteen. He looks down at the floor now and it's like he wants to leave.

"This isn't my choice either," he says quietly, and I don't know what to say to him and suddenly I see more of Shey in him than I'd like to. It's like he wants to say something else, but he doesn't. He turns, pushes the gun onto his back once again, and walks away.

♣ ♣ ♣ ♣

It's quieter tonight. After a day like today, everyone's a bit more tired, more subdued. It's like the wind blows away our energy and our chatter. Deva ate with us, as we were the last to eat, before going back to the kitchen to clear up. Then Cass and I walked out here, to our spot, sitting so our backs were against the fence.

I absentmindedly draw my name in the red dust with my finger in curly writing like Mum taught me. Cass watches. There's a commotion by the doors of the bunkhouse, something going on, but here, we're safe.

"It doesn't look like anything," Cass says, "just shapes."

I smile softly, take her hand, and squish down her fingers so that only her forefinger is left. I write "Cass" with it in the dust next to my name.

"What does that mean?"

"That's you," I answer, letting go of her hand. "Cass."

She smiles.

"C . . . A . . . S . . . S . . ." She tries to copy it underneath as I watch. She concentrates hard, and even though her *A* is a bit wobbly, I smile.

"So, what does it feel like?" she asks.

"What?"

"Reading?"

I shrug. "It's like . . ." I run out of words, frown. "It's like living a hundred lives," I say. Cass looks at me, her eyes widening.

"It's like you can see, smell, feel things you never thought you'd feel."

I can feel my stomach tightening when I think about it, that horrible nervousness that's there when you talk about things that you really love.

"You can be more than just yourself, you know?"

Cass looks confused. "I think so."

I exhale, brush my hands together to get rid of the dust. I look at the soil for a moment.

"Mum . . ." I try to steady my voice, take control of it. "Mum said she realized that the world was ending not when the starvations happened or the refugees, but when they started burning books."

Cass smiles at me and then the commotion on the other side of the yard gets louder. I look up, Cass does too. On the other side of the fence, some of the guards have gathered, and instead of having their backs to the yard like they're supposed to, they're watching what's going on. There's raucous laughter from some shrieking girls, and the unmistakable voice of Charmian.

"She's a four for sure," she says, her voice high and girly. She's singled out a girl, Maisie, I think, they're all standing around her.

"What are they doing?" whispers Cass.

"I don't know," I answer, getting up. Cass does the same and brushes the dust off her dress. "It's time for bed anyway," I say.

We walk around the crowd, trying not to look, trying to slip around them unnoticed, but I see a familiar shape through the fence—O'Brien. Unlike the other guards, his back's still turned like it should be, but I would recognize him anywhere. And then comes her voice like an axe. Brutal. Sharp.

"Jess! The boys here say I'm a ten out of ten!" Some of the guards laugh and I stop in my tracks.

"Come on," I whisper to Cass. I start walking away, Cass by my side, then to my horror Charmian comes through the crowd and starts to pull on my arm. Enraged, I try to shake her off.

"Jess! Jess! Jess!" The chanting starts.

"Come on, Jess, it's just a game, you're such a mood killer. We want to get to know you a little bit. You've been here long enough. Don't you want to make friends?"

She's pulling me harder, dragging me, and suddenly I'm encircled, my cheeks burning. She steps back, her eyes flaming. Delighted.

"Come on! What do we think?" she asks the crowd. "Hasn't got many curves."

There's laughter now.

"She's so straight! She's gonna struggle to have babies."

It's like I can't see anything except a sea of faces and some of Charmian's friends holding Cass back, her face white, scared.

"Her waist's too thick, no shape at all."

I try to move but it's like I'm stuck to the spot.

"Skin's too white, no good in the sun, looks like she'll just get red and angry." More laughter. The boys are shouting now too.

"What about her top half?" The guards are whooping.

I can feel my heart beating now, it hurts, it really hurts.

"There's nothing there." The laughter is louder this time.

"And look at that hair!" Charmian's walking around me in a circle, a sudden hush from the girls, and her voice changes now too, it's oilier, crueler. "Traitor's hair, ugly hair."

She stops now and walks toward me, a curious smile on her face.

"That's the hair of someone who thought they were better than us. Someone who thought they could leave us all to work our fingers to the bone while she ran away. . . . It's selfish hair. It's hair that says 'I'll do what I want.' The funny thing is, though, that you're here with the rest of us, aren't you, Jess?"

I want to hit her, hit her hard. It's almost a reflex, like I can't control it, but I know that's what she wants.

"A girl who doesn't want to work, who doesn't want children. . . . I'd say she's a zero. A score of zero!"

The bell rings. Loudly. And for the first time ever, I'm glad to hear it.

"A big fat zero!" Charmian laughs and keeps staring at me as everyone else begins to leave. I won't let her have the satisfaction of thinking she's hurt me, so I stare back until eventually she laughs again and makes her way into the bunkhouse. Everyone else leaves too, not that I can see much of them, there's nothing in front of me but a sea of blurred colors. Cass comes over, red marks on her wrists where she was held back. She doesn't need to say anything, she just hugs me tight until I almost can't breathe before we're shouted at by the guards.

5.

"Stop!" I shout at Shey. "Come back!"

He's running down the street, looking back over his shoulder at me. He's laughing and I can't catch him because his legs are longer. We're playing tag and he ducks behind a derelict house. He's so fast. I can't quite see where he's gone, my hair is in my face, and I pull it away, and then suddenly I glimpse him darting into an empty house, so I follow. My hand is on the doorframe, my breathing too fast. I look for him but there's nothing but the rubble on the floor, the plaster falling off the walls, bricks showing through, and there's another doorway, and I walk slowly toward it. . . .

"Shey! Don't hide!"

There's no answer.

"Shey? It's not funny anymore. . . ."

I can hear someone breathing, so I walk closer and closer toward the door and there's someone there, on the floor in a military uniform, and they've been shot, and their fingers are blue, their mouth open, and it's Shey. . . .

I wake up gasping. The wind is worrying the bunkhouse. I can't breathe. I get up, stand. I don't want to be under

Cass's bunk. I press my nails into my palms, I'm all right, I'm all right, I tell myself, it was just a dream. I try to get some relief from my breathing, but the air is warm and it's like I'm drowning. It's all quiet, everyone else is asleep. I try to focus on the floor, the lines in it. I look at the lines, I know where I am then, and I move to the window.

It's like the whole world is moving, the wind howling, and I watch as hundreds of pieces of paper swirl in the sky, tumbling in the gale, and suddenly I'm four years old again watching Mum go outside to gather as many up as she can. I see her running here and there, shuffling them in her hands and bringing them back inside, where we turn them over and practice our handwriting. Whenever there was deep unrest, they'd fly a helicopter over the city and plaster the place with images of General Porter, trying to ingrain his face into everyone and everything. After we had finished our lessons for the day, Mum would let Shey and me have a few spares and he'd make paper planes out of them and I'd shut myself in my room and draw with the pencil, disappear into myself and leave the house and the city and the world behind. As I look out now, I realize they must've dropped so many leaflets recently.

Ruth said that when storms used to happen when she was small, they were really exciting. I can't even imagine it. She said it used to happen only rarely, when it got really hot, and afterward there was this release, of heat, and of tension, she used to say, and it would start to rain, and then everything would start to grow, everything was renewed again. I've only ever known storms like this one. Red. Burning hot. No relief.

She said that there used to be distinct seasons too—four of them. That people looked forward to each one, celebrated them. Christmas and summer holidays. She said that there was certainty, that one followed the other, but I can't imagine the peace and the freedom of that.

There's still nothing except the wall of red dust and a few dots of lights—the security lights along the main wall where the guards' bunkhouses are. I turn back to bed. Cass is still sleeping, she was so tired. I lie back down again, back straight, legs out, in line with the bunks of girls all sleeping. Each one with her own story that nobody here wants to hear. Each one with her own dreams locked inside her head.

I'm not sure where Mum got the idea from, perhaps she talked to Ruth about it. The military was increasingly making random checks, knocking on the door to look at our paperwork. Mum would ask me to recite the fake date of birth on the identification card, and you could tell that they were skeptical, and I couldn't blame them. I knew my body was changing and it was harder to pretend I was under eleven years old. Mum would walk to the tap at the end of the street and get some water. You couldn't drink it without boiling it, but it was okay to wash with. I'd stand up in the bathroom, rub a cloth over myself, and I could feel my waist narrowing, these painful nubs where my chest was. Shey was changing too. His shoulders were getting broader, and his voice had deepened so that sometimes I'd feel scared when I heard him in the other room, thinking that someone had broken in, but it was just Shey, a different Shey. He stank of sweat in the heat too.

Ruth came over the day that Mum cut my hair, sat at the end of the table, her old face serious. Tense. She watched as Mum scraped my hair back into a ponytail and grabbed the old, blunt scissors. Mum's hands were shaking, trembling, and there was this strange scrunching noise as the dull edges of the scissors skewed through the thickness of my hair. She had to saw a little back and forth, squeeze the blades until eventually she had my ponytail in her hand, and I felt my short hair fall about my ears. I reached up to feel the cut edges. The shock of it. Ruth had her elbows on the table, her veined hands on the sides of her face now, knowing how risky this was, how serious it would be if we were caught. She nodded as Mum threw my ponytail away to the corner of the room before trimming my hair as short as she could. We all knew that only married women were allowed to cut off their hair.

That night we packed, Shey and me. Tried to get our story straight, and the next morning, it was time. Shey couldn't look at Mum and I just couldn't let her go. I wanted to smell her, to feel her, I wanted to look at her face and etch it into my mind. I stuffed all my drawings into my bag, and at the doorstep Mum told us that she'd come find us, that she wouldn't stop until she found us. I remember this look on her face, her clenched jaw—and I tried to capture the feeling of her arms around me. Then Ruth hugged her too and we left.

Looking back, it might've been possible to believe it if Shey and I didn't look so much alike. Our story was that we were newly married and that I was pregnant and that we were just going out of the city for medical treatment. Every time I think about it, it's like I've got a stone pressing on the base of my throat. We were standing there, and Ruth gave the guards at the checkpoint our false papers and tried to ask the guard about his uniform—anything to distract him—but there was this flicker in the guard's eyes, and he disappeared to show our paperwork to another soldier, and I could feel Shey crumbling by my side. I grabbed his hand to steady him, squeezed his fingers, but it was too late. The panic was all over his face, his knees were trembling, and suddenly I felt him snatch his fingers away and he just ran. . . .

I can't think about it. Even though he is older than me, I felt so sorry for him, so desperately sorry, and I can only really remember the noises. Shey screaming as he was tripped to the floor and dragged away, the sound of the soldier slapping Ruth across the face and then the clunk of the back of the truck closing on me.

Thank goodness for Cass. Because the next thing I knew, I was here, in the compound. Stripped, searched. They took my clothes, my paintings, gave me my uniform, and left me outside, and I was just sitting on the earth, all my words gone, disappeared. I couldn't even look up until I saw a pair of shoes in front of me, the dust-edged bottom of a long skirt, and the sound of someone coming to sit by my side. She rubbed my arm, told me she'd be there as long as I needed her. She still knows when I can't find the words, sits with me in silence when I can't seem to find my voice.

There was whispering when we came back to the bunkhouse last night. A coldness in the air despite the overwhelming heat. I felt everyone's eyes on me. It was almost as if the other girls hadn't made the connection between my short hair and my trying to get away, or if they had, they hadn't let it worry them. Three months have passed now and my hair is softening, but it's still a tell, a symbol, a reason to look at me with suspicion. Now Charmian had drawn everyone's attention to it, it was like they couldn't be seen ignoring it anymore.

It's dark now, really dark. The smudgy redness of outside choking any signs of dawn. Just the heavy sound of sleeping, until I hear footsteps. I look over at the doorway into the next room. There are shadows, two figures, one shorter than the other, a deep voice. It's Charmian, and a guard. I stare into the darkness, my hearing somehow heightened. They're very close and I'm sure he hands her something, which she pockets. She makes this girly noise that is not quite a laugh and I feel sick. I stay still and he sends her back to bed and I hear a door slide closed against the wind again. And then it's quiet once more, the strange interruption like it never happened, and I close my eyes and wait for morning.

6.

Cass has been sitting on my bed for ages, I feel her weight moving around as she chats with Deva. They're playing dominoes. I can hear Cass matching the patterns and Deva laughing sometimes, the wind still blowing outside. We won't go out today, even Father Renatus wouldn't send us out in this.

Deva is fifteen. She can't work up the ladders, not like the rest of us, because she has these fits sometimes and the drugs she needs are not always available, so they let her work in the kitchen, drag her to the side of the room if she has an episode and leave her to come around. She won't be allowed to marry; her best hope will be to stay here in the kitchens, be useful, and sometimes I don't know whether to feel sorry for her or to envy her.

I listen to the blocks clinking on the floorboards. The domino set is Cass's pride and joy and they have these really loud arguments about the game. Cass is convinced that dominoes is a game of blind luck, but Deva says that you have to strategize. I stretch, and Cass can feel that I'm awake, but she lets me come to slowly, my mind going back to last night—to the two figures and to Charmian's laugh and the passing of something from one to another.

"There's bread there," says Deva. I stretch and half smile at her. "You missed breakfast. Cass didn't want to wake you."

I touch Cass's arm in thanks as she concentrates on the dominoes, and I prop myself up on an elbow and start to eat, trying not to get crumbs on the mattress. Their hair is undone today, Cass's a deep auburn and Deva's two curtains of blue black. Deva sits on the floor, the domino pieces between her legs.

"No!" She smiles. "You big cheat!"

Cass smiles back.

"Nice try," Deva reproaches her.

I look up at the window. The chatter is growing inside the bunkhouse now.

"How long do you think this will last?" I ask.

Deva shrugs. "More rest I guess," she says, concentrating on her next move.

I lie back on the bunk. It could be days. Days penned up here with one another, everyone irritable, their suspicious eyes on me. My stomach sinks at the thought of it. Then the door opens and a Mother appears with a scarf around her face. Everyone snaps to, stands up. Deva and Cass too, the dominoes scattering between them, and I almost hit my head on the top bunk as I rush to get up. Mother Clement's face appears as the scarf falls down around her shoulders. She surveys us.

"I need a few volunteers," she says. Everyone does their best to shrink, to disappear.

She looks across the dorm. "Taylor?"

Katie Taylor nods.

"Coleman?"

Grace Coleman nods.

I see Mother Clement's eyes survey our faces, and with a strange desire to escape from here for a while, I put up my hand.

"Jess?" She sounds almost surprised. She scrutinizes me a moment before nodding imperceptibly. "Very well."

Cass looks at me, worried.

"I'll be okay," I mouth at her.

"Quickly, then," says Mother Clement, gathering the scarf around her face again.

I pull my work dress over my head, slip my feet into my shoes, and fall in line behind Grace. "Cover your mouths," Mother Clement says before opening the door.

The wind is brutal. Shocking. We shuffle forward, our shoulders shrugged as if it makes any difference. We wait, narrow our eyes so the dirt doesn't get in them, and watch as she fights to close the door again, our skirts tugged violently by the wind. I try not to breathe too much through my nose, the abrasiveness of the sand burning my cheeks. I put my hand on Katie's shoulder so I can follow her across the yard where a guard unlocks a metal gate to let us through.

We follow Mother Clement behind the Assembly Hall now and across to another building I haven't seen before. Another guard opens the door as he sees us coming, and I can make out the name on his jacket as we walk in. O'Brien. The closing of the door is a shock, the sudden absence of noise. O'Brien locks the door behind us and ignores us as he's supposed to do. It takes us a while to come to our senses. Grace is coughing, so is Katie. We try to wipe the dust from our faces with our sleeves. It's like my lungs are lined with dirt, and then I look up.

There's a long narrow table laid out on the left and on it are what look like colored swatches of silk. I look again, narrow my eyes. It's not silk, it's different strands. It's hair.

Mother Clement shakes out her scarf, straightens out her skirts. "Since it's impossible to go out today, you'll be assembling brushes with the girls here."

There are around five girls already working. One I recognize as Xiao looks like she's washing the hair, another girl I don't know is using a penknife to straighten out and cut the knots off pieces of wood for handles, and a few others seem to be pinching fine amounts of hair, cutting it, and then gluing it to the wood before binding it with some sort of string.

"Taylor, you can wash. Coleman, go to woodwork. Jess, you can bind."

We nod and walk to our stations. There's a strong smell of chemicals here, the quiet concentration of people at work. The girl binding the brushes looks up as I approach. She doesn't smile.

"I'm Zuri," she says quietly, and I recognize her from Assembly.

"I'm Jess," I say, my voice breaking. I can't tear my eyes from the tables.

"It's not hard, don't worry," she says, trying to read my face.

"It's not that. It's just that I'd never thought about the brushes," I say, embarrassed.

She shrugs. "Why would you?"

She looks at me looking at the hair on the table. "We might as well use it," I hear her say, but I can't take it in, not really. I can't look away from the hair that has been cut and taken and the girls who left here to get married whether they wanted to or not.

7.

After three days the bunkhouse is raging inside and out, words are like tinder, arguments flaming over the smallest of things. Even though most of us have nothing, some of the girls barter things. That's where most of the arguing comes from, from exchanging things they have been given by guards. Food. Combs. Hair wax. I don't know what they do to get them, but Cass said that some of them pass information to the guards in return for favors, so it's best not to trust anyone. She says other things go on too, but I don't want to know about it.

    I listen as Cass hums in the bunk above and I think about the brushes. I've dreamed of them every night since working on them. I feel embarrassed about the way I felt comforted by them when I first came here, how they reminded me of being at home painting. The strange betrayal of knowing that they're made of our hair. I hear Cass as she turns over on her side, looks out the window. She's quiet today, thoughtful. I told her and Deva about the brushes but not about the hair, I don't know if Cass knows, but I don't want to be the one to tell her.

"Jess?" she asks.

"Mmm?"

I can almost hear her thinking.

"If they look at you, and match you with someone so you have a good chance of having a healthy baby, what are the chances that you'll actually like them?" Her voice sounds fragile as glass.

"Same as liking anyone, I suppose. . . . ," I say, my eyes following hers to the red dust clouds outside.

"But do you think there's more of a chance because you're so matched biologically?"

"I don't think it works like that," I say, although I haven't really thought that much about it. I know she's resting her head on her hands now, both of them under her cheek, her palms together. She always does that when she's thinking.

"I . . . I . . . don't think there's room for"—I feel silly saying it—"love, if that's what you're thinking?" I imagine her cheeks flushing the faintest shade of pink as she looks out at the endless red landscape, her cheek crinkled against her hands.

"I suppose not," she says quietly. "I don't suppose there's a point to it. But you said people wrote about it?"

"All the time," I say.

"And it was important?"

"I think so."

I don't know what she wants me to say. I could tell her that people wrote about it like it was more important than life itself, but that wouldn't help. I could tell her that I've been trying to imagine what color it is, but that wouldn't comfort her either.

"I wonder what it feels like," she says quietly.

I think for a moment. "I don't know."

The thing is, though, that I do kind of know what it might feel like, and I want to tell her, but I can't because it sounds so stupid and I've never told anyone, not even Mum. It's just that sometimes, at the weirdest moments, sometimes not even when I am at my happiest or when someone's done something nice, it can be at the worst time, or in the strangest place; but sometimes, I have this intense feeling of love, for everyone and everything.

When I was at home, I'd be looking out the bars of the window, and I'd see someone carrying a child, and I'd feel this connection, this warmth, or this stupid love for our pathetic selves. It would happen with Ruth too, when she'd show me the books she'd brought over for me, or when she'd ask me to comb her hair, and I would stand behind her and see her scalp through her thinning hair and the softness of her old skin, and I would feel this heartbreaking love. Even Shey, I could feel his fear, the way he could never look you in the eyes.

It doesn't make sense. To love something so broken. To love things that are imperfect and messed up and damaged, but I do, and it's the most delicate coral pink, and this sap rising fizzy green, and the sootiest deep charcoal that edges a butterfly wing.

Suddenly there's a figure by my bunk. "Get up," she spits. It's Charmian. I hadn't even noticed her come over.

Cass jerks up to sitting, swings her legs over the bunk. I get up, feeling vulnerable lying down.

Charmian's looking at me coolly. "Give me the dominoes."

I feel my stomach sink. "They're Cass's," I say.

"Give them to me."

I can feel the room go quiet around us. Cass slips off the bunk and lands barefoot on the floor.

"Traitors don't deserve nice things," Charmian says, not taking her eyes off me. I can feel my stomach tighten.

"Didn't you hear me? I said they're Cass's. And they're the only thing she's got."

Charmian takes her time. "What a shame," she sneers.

Cass turns to slide the box from under her mattress. "It's okay—" she begins.

"Don't, Cass," I interject.

Cass looks at me, not knowing what to do, her eyes darting everywhere. I know it's not worth it, I know Charmian thrives on this, but I can't help myself. There are girls moving closer now, sensing the tension.

"Got anything to trade?" I ask.

She smirks, laughs, then her mouth straightens.

I take my time now. "You must have *something* to trade? I don't know, maybe you picked something from a guard?"

Her eyes harden in realization. "The thing about you," she says steadily, "is you don't know what you're talking about." She moves closer. "You think you're better than us, don't you?" she says. "You think you're cleverer?"

I can feel my heart clenching and unclenching, her warm breath on my cheek. She studies my face unnervingly, and I can feel myself waver.

"You thought you could beat the system, didn't you?"

There's coldness to her laughter now. She tilts her head

as if she feels sorry for me. "Are you really that stupid? The only way to beat the system is to be in it." Her eyes are blazing now. "You're nothing but scum."

I don't see it coming. It's a shock, like a loud noise next to you. She grabs my hair and smacks my head into the metal bunk behind me, knocking my temple. Cass leaps forward but she's too late. For once there isn't frenzied shouting, just some half-suppressed laughing as a trickle of blood slides down past my eye. I look back, dazed, and watch as Charmian smirks, satisfied, takes the dominoes, and walks away.

8.

The guard comes in with Mother Clement this morning and that can mean only one thing. She stands behind him as he clears his throat.

"Nadia Polek, you have been matched with Bryce Olly."

"Grace Coleman, you have been matched with Frank Naseby."

"Fia O'Lynn, you have been matched with Nathan Williams."

He looks across at Mother Clement. "That's it for this bunkhouse."

There's a palpable sense of relief as he turns and leaves. The girls whose names have been called look around at their friends, they knew it was coming from the moment they got their period, from when the swabs were taken from their mouths in the medical room to test their genes for potential illnesses, but you can still sense their tension.

"Girls for the Brush House please," Mother Clement says, and stands waiting for us.

I get up, my head still aching. The cut has crusted over with black blood, but my temple is swollen, and I can kind of see it from the edge of my vision. Last night Cass sat on the floor of the bathroom with me and pressed her rag to it until it stopped bleeding. Then we sat in silence not knowing what to say. I follow Katie to the door, worried to be leaving Cass on her own, and to my relief, I see Deva walking over to her bunk. I keep my head down as I walk past Mother Clement.

"Stop," she says. I feel myself shrink, her gray eyes on me. "Turn around."

I know there's no point arguing.

"What happened?"

I think a moment, see Cass reach out for Deva's arm in the corner of my eye, and say, "I fell, Mother."

She narrows her eyes, and I know I'm entirely at the mercy of her mood. She looks tired, her curiosity flattening quickly to boredom, and to my relief, she shrugs and looks away.

I follow the others through the relentless wind, cupping my hand over my temple so it doesn't sting as much. We know where we're going now and can follow one another's footsteps without having to lift our heads to look up. It is still hot, dry, there seems to be no end to it. As the door closes behind us, as we walk across to the gluing station, I look up and feel a strange relief to be here.

Zuri showed me how to gather the hair, how to graduate it and glue it all around the wooden handle before binding it around with some string made from synthetic plastic. The trick was to turn the brush, not the string, otherwise you'd get in a tangle. She spent a whole morning teaching me, my hands in hers, as she turned the brush in her fingers, and I had to ask her again and again to slow down. Eventually I got the hang of it and made one from scratch on my own, and I looked up at her, neither of us knowing whether or not to smile at such a victory.

She looks up now, her eyes darting to my temple and away again as if she doesn't want to pry. The room is blissfully quiet compared to the bunkhouse. Mother Clement stays awhile before leaving us with the guards. O'Brien seems always to be here, and another older one called Hajek, whom I haven't seen before. I wait for more handles and go to the corner to wash my hands in alcohol to melt the glue, which sticks to your fingers. O'Brien looks up from his seat nearby, he nods his head, and I ignore him, turn away, and go back to my brushes.

I can still remember the first time I held a paintbrush; I was four and a half and I thought they were huge. Mum had watched me draw on the back of the leaflets and had bartered for this set of dried-out paints—a dented tin around the size of a brick, and inside were squares of something that all looked exactly the same color. I remember her opening the box in front of me and then licking her finger and rubbing the colors back to life. They were labeled Burnt Umber, Titanium White, Sap Green, Cyan, Van Dyke Brown, Prussian Blue, Midnight Black. And I thought it was magic, how you could add a little water and spread them out like that, and even though they were old and dry, you could just bring them back to life and make something new out of them. Mum said I slept with the brush that night, wouldn't let it go. I find myself holding a brush and dipping it into a tin of water nearby and instinctively drawing with water on the table. I look up and notice

O'Brien watching me. I frown, put the brush down again, and Grace passes me some more handles.

The first brushes Mum gave me were hard. Someone had painted with them and then left them without washing them. I had to tease every fiber out of the stiff nib. One by one. And then one day Mum showed me how to create different effects with them. She'd laugh and say, "I should be teaching you survival skills, not painting," and I'd laugh too.

Zuri finishes another brush and goes to wash her hands, and I can't stop myself. I pick up a finished brush and dip it in water again and watch as the waves of the sea appear on the table for a moment. Then, as the water dries, they disappear and I feel myself disappearing too. Not from myself but from here. There's a deep relief, and for the first time since I got here, I feel tears come to my eyes. Now. Here. Of all places. I put the brush back down and shake my head angrily. It's so stupid. Of all the things, it's *this* that makes me cry. I look up and see O'Brien looking at me again, and I could almost shout at him, but he looks away immediately. I turn, go, and wash my hands again as the other guard starts watching me. I rub the alcohol into my hands over and over until it stings and glance up and out through the bars on the window. My skin is red, my head hurts, and everything just feels raw, but as I look across the camp, the view is clearer.

The wind has dropped; we'll be out brushing tomorrow.

♣ ♣ ♣ ♣

"I can't believe the flowers survived," I say. It feels impossible that such delicate-looking things could be so indestructible.

"They're fine here too," Cass says from the other side of the tree. She starts to brush. "How did they withstand it?"

It is cooler today. There's no relief, like the relief Ruth talked about, but there's something, a change.

"I suppose they just held tight." I smile at Cass, and she smiles back, and I realize that she looks happier today. Perhaps the rest has done her good. It's quiet today too, nothing but a light breeze and the sound of the girls in the other trees, a kind of hum.

"Who do you think gets to eat apples?" Cass asks absent-mindedly, her arm moving among the flowers. I shrug; she brushes some more.

"Have you ever even seen one?"

I wonder what to say for a moment, thinking whether it's a story I can tell. "Yes," I say simply.

Cass stops brushing, confused, then she smiles. "You have?" She looks at me, tips her head slightly to the side in a question. "Really?"

"Keep brushing," I say, and she does, but without taking her eyes off me.

"It was Shey's birthday. He was twelve. Mum went to the ration line, like, every Monday, but she was so long coming back. I was worried and went to sit by the window. We waited and waited for what seemed like forever, and she came walking really fast along the road, and she had her bag pressed under her elbow like this." I motion it to Cass and her eyes widen.

"I ran to the door to open it and she pushed past me, and she looked almost wild with excitement. I locked the door and walked to the kitchen and she put her bag down and she had two apples." I can feel Cass's astonishment radiating from her. She's brushing slower without even realizing it.

"We had to sing 'Happy Birthday' to Shey, and she let us hold them and smell them first. And then she let me draw them. They were green, but like lots of shades of green with reddish flecks on them, and around the stalks there were these matte brown patches by the curve where the stalk went."

I can see Mum's face now. The way she presented them to Shey after I finished painting them, and Shey asking if we could share them, and then the time it took to decide how to split them three ways.

"And Shey wanted to share," I say, "but he felt bad for Ruth, the old woman who lived next door, so Mum went to get her. Mum always kept a knife in the back waistband of her pants, and she pulled it out and she sliced them really, really thinly so we could get all the flavor out of them." I can feel my smile fading.

"And what was it like?" asks Cass.

"Sweet, sharp, a bit sour, but fresh, like you could taste something alive."

Cass looks at me in disbelief, a smile on her face. Such a smile that I couldn't tell her about how Shey burst out crying after finishing eating and licking his fingers to get all the juice. About how he suddenly realized that he was a year older and a year closer to having to leave, and I tear my mind away from his hand disappearing from mine and him being tackled to the floor.

"It really was something," I say quietly.

"You two all right?" comes a voice, and Cass almost falls off her ladder. Both our minds were so far away, we didn't hear footsteps. It's O'Brien.

"We're fine, thank you," answers Cass, suddenly tense again.

"I think you need water," he says.

I look over at Cass. Shake my head imperceptibly. "No, thank you," I say firmly.

"No, I think you need water, especially you," he says to me. "Come here."

He's looking at me. I freeze. He waits.

"I said now."

I've got no choice. That's an order and you cannot ignore orders. I place the brush into my apron pocket and grip the edges of the ladder and slowly find each rung with my feet. I look around, everyone's busy. I walk toward him, and he pulls the canteen of water over his head again. He offers it to me.

"I don't want it," I say. I expect him to order me, I expect him to force me.

"You don't have to," he says quietly, and suddenly he looks unsure. "At least hold the flask, will you?" I take hold of the water and he takes something from his pocket. He looks scared.

"I thought you might like these."

I can't see what they are. I try to give him back the water and he presses a small material bag of something into my hand.

"Put them in your apron," he says. Surprised, I do what he says. I can't think. Then he nods and walks away. I watch him go a moment and then turn, walk back to the bottom of the ladder, and climb up slowly, the unfamiliar weight of whatever is in the package against the tops of my legs as I climb.

Cass is staring at me. "What is it?"

"I don't know," I say. "I can't look now. We'll have to wait."

Cass can barely contain herself. I put my hand in my apron pocket and take out my brush and start to work. A dread grows inside me, one for what I've just taken from him, and two because as I've gotten more used to his face, he doesn't seem to have the superiority that the other guards have. He looks young too, and scared.

9.

"It's paint," I whisper.

Cass is outside the stall waiting for me, I can see her feet on the floor under the door.

I spread the tubes out on my palms. Five small cylinders of paint about the length of my fingers, the labels are rubbed off. I place four of them on the closed toilet and unscrew one of them. They're still sealed. I hold the tube in my hands and then I realize that I'm shaking. Cass has stayed outside in case someone comes in.

"They're soft, unopened."

"Why did he?"

I stop, think, and answer, "I'm not sure, but he's in the Brush House, perhaps he saw me with the brushes."

Cass goes quiet, I go quiet, an unasked question on both sides of the door. The shadows of Charmian and the guard flick through my mind. I look at the paints once again and feel this almost unbearable yearning to open them, to fetch my brush, but I can't. I stuff them back into my apron and stand in silence a moment.

"I'll give them back to him," I say, and although Cass doesn't answer, I know she understands.

I open the door and two other girls come in. Cass pretends to use the toilet and I wash my hands with a rag. We wait for the girls to leave, and Cass turns to me. "It was kind of him."

"You think?" I ask. "Unless he wants something in return."

"I don't think he's like that. . . ."

"Cass . . ."

She looks crestfallen. "But you love painting. . . . ," she says, looking pained.

"I'll give them back to him. It's safer," I say again, trying to keep my voice level.

"Of course," she replies. "Of course." She shakes her head and then the bell rings and we have to go and eat.

"Come on," she says, linking her arm in mine, and we walk to the Food Hall side by side, Cass deep in thought and me feeling like everyone can see the paint through my apron.

"Just act normal," whispers Cass, feeling how tense my body is, and then, "I know how difficult that is for you."

I can't help but smile, and we join the back of the queue.

Deva's here tonight again and she winks at Cass. She always gives us a little bit more. Not enough to make the other girls complain, but just a little bit. I walk over to the farthest table, away from everyone else, and Deva finishes her shift and comes to sit with us. I eat, trying to wash down the dry bread with the bitter water, and listen as Deva and Cass speak to each other, but I can't concentrate. The weight of the paint in my lap is distracting me. I can't bear having it so near to me and not be able to use it, and the more I think about it, the angrier I get—at O'Brien for reading me like that and putting us both in a position where we could get into real trouble. I get up, tip what's left on my plate onto Cass's.

"You okay?" she looks up.

I nod. "I just need to do something."

Deva looks confused but Cass nods, puts her hand on Deva's as she begins to ask questions, which silences her.

I walk out of the hall past the tables of girls, each one palpably quieting down as I walk past. The cut on my temple has mellowed into bruising now, reaching from the side of my eye all the way down to the middle of my cheek. I reach the door and walk to the exercise yard. I don't know if he's there, so I scan the perimeter. I can't see him, so I walk to my usual spot, sit with my back to the fence, and look at the space in the middle of the yard where Charmian pulled me, and for a moment, I can hear them all laughing again, and I feel sick.

Perhaps I am a traitor, because I would definitely leave. I would leave every sorry one of them to fend for themselves. I don't want to end every day exhausted from doing something so mindlessly pointless because the men who came before us only thought about their today. I don't want to have a baby just to replace the numbers. Perhaps there should . . . perhaps there should be a last baby, just like that last bee. And perhaps the best thing for us would be to tip the balance once again and in one generation for us to disappear completely because we're not worthy of this place because we're so stupid and selfish and now these paints in my apron feel like bombs and the stupid boy who gave them to me is not even here. I just want to scream.

It's getting dark now, and I see Cass and Deva in the distance walking, chatting, and as I just about think of getting up, I hear footsteps behind me. I don't look back, but I know it's him, I can feel it. I feel my jaw set. I get the paints out of my apron and put them behind my back, then I slowly push them toward the wire netting.

"Take them," I say, trying to keep my voice even. "I don't want anything from you."

He doesn't move. He probably has his back to me too. There's nothing, no movement, no voice. Nothing.

"I'm sorry," he says eventually. "I thought . . . I'm sorry, I could've got you into trouble."

I listen to his voice.

"If you leave them there, I'll pull them through when it's dark."

I nod; that's that, then. I think about getting up but then I can't. I sit in silence for a painful amount of time.

"My father was a musician," he says quietly. "He had a guitar."

I don't know what to say, my palms resting on the red dust, listening, watching the yard getting darker.

"Mum said that he used to lay me on top of it when I was a newborn, in the curve in the top, and strum these chords, and that'd stop me crying."

There's a tightness in my chest now. Something in his voice, a kind of key change that makes me not want to know how the story ends.

"When I was thirteen, this gang broke in, they took my Mum to another room, killed her. Stole the guitar. And it was like they took a way of speaking from him. He locked everything inside and he hardly spoke again. It kind of broke him. I . . . I just saw something similar in your eyes when you had those brushes."

There's a silence now that's deeper than indigo.

"Anyway," he says, trying to loosen up his voice a little, "I really am sorry." I hear his feet start to move.

"Wait," I say. I can hear him stop.

"I don't want anything from you," he says. "I hope you understand that."

It's strange, but I believe him.

"It's important you know that," he says again. "It's just, I thought you needed them."

"Thank you, O'Brien."

"It's Eliot."

"I'm Jess," I say.

There's another brief moment's pause before the bell rings. Then I put my hand behind me, feel for the paints, and take them back.

10.

The gates scrape open along the soil, the same jeering, the same whoops from the guards. I turn away and look at Cass. She sat close to me at breakfast today, hasn't left my side. She closes her eyes now and we both listen to the engine.

I watched her undress last night. When I first arrived three months ago, she used to walk around in her vest, talking, gesticulating wildly about this and that, but now she crosses her arms, jumps into bed quickly after pulling her dress up over her head. She's changing and seems painfully aware of it. I'm changing too. We all have a clock to sixteen and each day is counting down, although they'll take a girl even younger than that sometimes, if they think medically she'll be able to have a child. I look around, the girls' thin faces staring, their hair tied back tightly, a certain hollowness to their eyes. We travel the rest of the way in silence.

I close my eyes and think about the paints hidden under my mattress. There are two black tubes, one brown, red, and green. Last night I waited until everyone had settled down and hid them under my washrag to walk to the bathroom. I locked myself in a stall, and as I opened the cloth, I realized my hands were shaking. I studied the Midnight Black first, turned it over in my hands, and even though I really tried not to, I had to open it. Breathe it in. The sulfur smell mixed with a strange sweetness. The texture oily and glossy, and strangely it wasn't just the preciousness of having something for myself. It wasn't having the *paint* that woke something up inside me, it was having an idea, owning a few possibilities, and I realize now that Mum was right. She'd never had to brush inside the camps, so she didn't know how to prepare me, but she said that it was important to find something to hold on to, to give yourself options. To never believe your path was set one way, and it's the same with colors, because you may have only three or four, but if you mix them, blend them, you can create more and more, and if you keep going, your choices in the end are infinite. If you could create a portrait of someone in shades of one color only so that there was light and shade and life, the possibilities with *more* than one color were boundless.

The driver bangs the butt of his gun on the side of the truck, bringing me sharply back to today, and the girls start to file off. I slip in behind a girl from the next dorm and start to walk toward the back of the truck. Cass falls in behind me. It is hot today. Still. A kind of stillness that tries to drown you. I walk with Cass to the trees, pick a ladder, and get to work. We work in silence, Cass looking over at me every now and again. The hours pass in scorching heat, and I can feel the sweat beading down my back.

"What did he say when you gave them back?" Cass asks. I keep brushing, scan the bottom of the trees for guards. "I didn't," I say.

"You didn't what? You didn't talk to him?" Cass frowns.

"I didn't give them back," I answer, my voice steady.

She stops brushing now, stares at me in wide-eyed astonishment. "But what are you going to—" she begins. A guard has turned, is walking this way.

"Shshshsh," I warn her, and she looks over her shoulder, keeps reluctantly quiet. We wait until he walks past us.

"The dorms could be searched, someone else could find them," she whispers through her teeth.

"I know," I say. "It's just that I can't let them go yet."

She looks at me. "Are you sure he doesn't want anything from you in return?"

"No." I shake my head. "It's nothing to do with Eliot," I say firmly. "It's to do with me."

She looks at me, carries on brushing. "But what are you going to do with them?"

I shrug. "I don't know, it's just that . . ." And I don't know how to explain. "It's just that I feel like they were meant for me?" She's looking at me now with those blue eyes and I know she accepts it, accepts what I said, along with everything else that doesn't make sense to her about me. She nods and we work in silence.

"Tell me about what your Mum said," she asks after a while, the sun beating down on us both.

I give her a soft smile. "I don't know what you're talking about," I tease.

Cass fixes me with a fake glare. "It's my favorite story," she says. "Please . . ."

I smile. "You could recite it to me," I say.

"But it's better when you tell it," she pleads.

I wait a moment, clear my throat, and keep brushing, my eyes squinting against the harsh light. "She says that they're starting a new community in the North, that there are species there, surviving, starting to thrive."

Cass listens, rapt, even though she's heard it a million times before.

"And that they're rekindling the ecosystem and that there are animals and everyone's free to do as they please but they choose to help one another."

She has this look on her face, the same one I had when listening to Ruth talking about the theater plays and films she saw as a young woman.

"There's no brushing?"

I tilt my head. "A little brushing, but you never know, they might find some wild bees one day."

Her face is soft now, restful. "It's a great story, isn't it?" she says.

I swallow my spit, my mouth dry. "But what if it's not a story?" I ask. Her eyes dart to mine.

"What if it's true?" I say.

She looks unsure now and I can feel her difficulty in imagining that it might be real. "Do *you* think it's true?" she asks.

I remember asking Mum the same question, whether her friends had really made it out, whether they'd really started again in a valley somewhere. I had the same look in my eyes as Cass has now, and without flinching, Mum would answer as I do now. "Yes," I say simply, "it's got to be."

I watch Cass struggle, pushing out the edges of her mind.

"I don't know," she says quietly. "It would be lovely, though. Wouldn't it?"

♣ ♣ ♣ ♣

At the end of the day, we get back on the truck, drive back to the camp, and my mind is still on the North, still on the paints, as I get to the bottom steps of the truck—so I don't realize what's happening when the girl in front swings her foot behind her, sending me flying onto the ground face-first. I land heavily, gasp in shock, breathe in some dust, and start to cough.

"Jess!" I hear Cass's heavy feet on the metal steps. I can feel her beside me.

"Why did you do that?" Cass shouts, her voice breaking in anger.

I get up to sitting. "I'm all right, Cass," I cough.

"No, you're not!" she shouts. "Why would you do that?" she asks the fair-haired girl again. She just looks at Cass and shrugs. I hold my chest—cough and cough. There's mucus and dust on my palms. The guard comes over and pushes his way toward us. "What's going on?" he asks impatiently. I try to swallow down the coughing.

"She tripped her," says Cass accusingly.

The girl looks at the guard, shows her upturned palms, shrugs. "I was just walking down, she must've slipped. Not my fault she can't even walk properly."

"Get up," says the guard roughly. "I said, get up."

Cass tries not to mutter as she hauls me to my feet, and

the girls begin to disperse, winding their way through the fence toward the bunkhouses, the fair-haired girl walking arm in arm with Charmian.

Cass helps to brush me off. "You really okay?" she asks.

I nod, still winded.

"Come on," she says, pulling my arm, "let's go wash."

I follow her, and it's not just my face that's stinging, it's the fact that some of the girls are getting crueler. The fact that there was no laughter this time, or shocked giggles. When I fell, there was just silence and a deafening indifference.

I watch as the red dust runs down my legs into the drain with the water. There's a burn on my knee, where I fell, and the water stings the side of my cheek. We get one bowl of water morning and night and you have to make it stretch as far as you can. When it got hotter, lakes ran dry, water got scarce, they had to dig deeper and deeper for it. They realized how valuable it was and started bartering access to water, and that's when they started to ration it.

I dry myself and for the first time in a while I feel my hair tickling my shoulders. It's growing again and perhaps I should be happy about that, that it'll make me more like them, but I hate it. It's a daily reminder of how long I've been here. I pull on my vest, rub my teeth with a rag. There's only one mirror, cracked and blotchy with rust. I haven't looked at myself in months. Not really. I peer at the shattered reflection of myself now, and for a moment I swear I see my mother looking back at me. Her brown hair, her thin face in mine. I gasp, grab the stand, and steady myself.

Once women raise children and once those children have been taken away to fight or brush, the regime no longer finds them useful. By forty most of them can't have any more children, so they have to work in manual jobs like irrigation, or if they can read and write, doing paperwork for the military. After that or if they get ill, they're on their own.

I don't know what Mum will do, because I know it's not in her nature to follow orders—to do what she's told. I know that she can't not tell the truth, and I love that about her, but it also scares me, and as I look in the mirror and see a younger version of her in myself, I hear her promise to come and find us, and she meant it, I know she did. But I also know that it's impossible. I can't think of her too much, because what worries me the most is that I don't know if she even knows what happened. I don't know if Ruth got home that night after being slapped. I worry that if she didn't, Mum might still have hope. She might still imagine us out there, outside the border, outside the wall, free, whatever that means, and perhaps she went looking for us.

Someone's banging on the screen. I throw my washrag over my shoulder and breathe, breathe, trying to block everything out until I'm ready to walk to my bunk. Once Mum creeps into my mind, it's hard to push her out. They're banging again. I straighten myself up and walk out, make my way back to the bunk. I lie down and wait for the dorm to settle.

I don't blame the girl who tripped me up. Mum said it was human nature, that once someone was pushed out, you didn't associate with them in case you were pushed out too. It was about survival she said, the only thing was that those who were pushed out were sometimes the ones who found their own direction, did something new. My whole body is aching, the adrenaline still coursing in my blood, and it feels impossible to think of anything else except the way the water swirled down the drain just now and the turning inward of everything, and I close my eyes and listen as Cass hums to herself, and the way it quiets down everyone else, makes them sleepy.

Perhaps they were sung to too? And if they weren't, maybe their mothers were, or their mother's mothers were, and there's a memory somewhere in their minds or their hearts or their DNA. If the collapse taught us anything, it was that things are more complicated than we could ever imagine. I feel my body getting heavy from my feet to my legs, and I feel myself not knowing what's real and what's not, and that's when I see something like a kaleidoscope, something Ruth had in her house, and the colors all merge and separate and merge again, and then I sleep for a while before startling awake as usual.

11.

It's that time again in the middle of the night, and I can't breathe, and the thoughts keep coming down the tracks again and it's like I'm not even in my body, like I've left myself behind. My throat is tightening as if I'm choking. I was dreaming of the brush and what Father Renatus and this place have made it into—how we're not using the brushes for what they were meant for and how they're not letting us be what we're meant to be.

My hearing sharpens along the dirty, hard floors, and I push myself up on my elbow and listen. Listen. It's deadly quiet, so I sit up. I reach out through the shadows and pull my apron up from the bottom of the bed. I can feel the brush through the material, and I push my fingers into the pocket toward it. I hold it in my fingers and it looks like any other brush but it isn't. Brushes weren't meant to be made of girl's hair, brushes weren't meant to be used for pollinating. My hands go to the pillow, and I take out the paints, the tubes cool in my palm, and I sit a moment. There is no truth in the brush—that's what Ruth said about painting. She told me that when she watched me learning to sketch that there was a man who said that paintings were the lie that makes us realize the truth, and I suddenly feel like she told me that for a reason. And I don't know what I'm doing, but I find myself gathering the paints in my palm, reaching for my washrag, folding it over my hand so the paints are hidden. Then I drop my feet to the cold floor.

My skin is instantly covered in goose bumps. Every sense heightened. All the girls are sleeping, no sound except the occasional murmur as girls talk in their sleep, and I can't believe it, but I'm standing up among the bunks, trying to keep my breathing quiet. I look over toward the doorway out to the exercise yard and start to shift my weight, place one foot in front of the other carefully, quietly, until I get to the doorway. I look across to see Mother Jackson sitting on a chair in the adjoining dorm next door, her head to the side, she's sleeping. My heart is thumping now, I can hear it beating in my ears as I reach out and pull the handle. Slide it to one side and I feel the cooler air on my legs as I open it just enough to squeeze through and slip outside.

I gasp. I haven't been outside at night in forever. The moon is bright, making the red earth look black, and it's so quiet. Just the expanse of the landscape punctuated by dots of feeble solar lights and the stars up above. I've never seen them like this before, only through windows and bars—Mum would never risk taking us outside at night. I feel this tightness in my throat, and I realize it's tears. Tears pressing there. The stars are breathtaking, the scale, stretching on as far as the eye can see, and the only thing that I can think of is how unchanged they are. Unchanged since my mother was born. Unchanged since my grandmother was born. Steady since the earth began.

I realize I haven't breathed in about a minute and my stomach is clenched, so I press my free palm to it and try to control my breathing. Try to concentrate. I stay in the shadows, walk barefoot along the building, cross to the fence behind the bunkhouse. It's around twelve feet tall, a metal mesh, and along the top runs this length of spiky wire. I look around, but it's impossible to see much from here. If I get over the fence, there's a sixty-foot gap across a dirt road to the nearest part of the outer wall.

I wait, try to listen, sense a blurring of light in the darkness. I know the guards patrol at night, I've seen their torches move slowly across the scratched window of the dorms when I'm lying awake. Have counted the seconds from one light to the next, around one thousand two hundred seconds, every twenty minutes give or take. I wait as the light gets stronger and stronger. Hold my breath and try to push thoughts of *What the hell am I doing?* out of my mind. I wait for the light to pass; I can't see much from this angle. He must have gone, and I know I can't waste more time, I have to be over and back before the next guard comes. I will just have to trust that there's no one there. I think about what Mum would do and I decide that I have no choice. I have to move right now.

I drape the rag around my neck, shove the brush inside the side of my underwear, and clutch the paints in my hand, cling to the netting with the tips of my fingers, trying to find footholds in the mesh. It rattles a little with my weight, and I try to climb smoothly, in a straight line without tugging and hauling at it too much. Up I go, my arms strong from brushing, and without the skirt, the dress, the damned dress, I can move freely. It's like being a kid again. I reach the top, my arms shaking as I slip under the string of barbed wire that glistens brutally in the soft moonlight. My hair catches in the wire, and I pull at it, smooth it down, but as I do, a tube of paint drops from my hand and falls down the inside of the fence. My throat tightens, and I try not to swear. I can't see it through the darkness. As I swing my leg over, I hang on the top of the fence, try to work my feet down so I'm vertical again, and tense my shoulders and fingers so I can drop down in a controlled way on the other side.

I turn around, scan the bottom of the fence, see the fallen tube lying five inches inside the netting. I walk toward it, hunker down, and push my fingers into the mesh until they're jammed by the size of the opening, the tips of my fingers brushing the tube, feeling the sweat on my back despite the coolness, a panic setting in. I put down the other tubes, try again, try to scissor my forefingers to grasp the flat bottom edge of the tube, and I feel myself moving it. I peer through the dark, pull it toward me, maneuver it through. I gather the paints again, get up, every inch of my body aching, and turn to look at the wall behind me. My eyes are getting used to the darkness now, and I realize that the smudges in the sky I thought were clouds are formations of stars farther away. I can't hear anything, so I begin to walk, my heart in my mouth, across the expanse of space between the wire fence and the outer wall.

There's nowhere to hide now, nothing to give me shadow

to move in. And I feel a peace: if I am caught, then I am caught.

I move as quickly as I can, and suddenly the wall looms above me. So big it would be impossible to scale, but that's not what I want with it. In the darkness, under the aching stars, it's nothing but a canvas. An endless, perfect, smooth blank canvas.

I stand for a moment, feeling more alive than I have ever done, my hands shaking as I unscrew the tubes and start to paint.

12.

"Jess!" I can feel Cass near. "Jess!"

There's a commotion. I try to open my eyes, my arms aching, my legs stiff.

"Jess!" Her voice is on a knife edge. My mind focuses, suddenly pin sharp, my eyes snapping open.

She looks at me, her hands on my arms. She can't say what she wants to say, but it's all in her eyes.

"Something's happened. . . ." She emphasizes the "something." The dorm is thick with voices. But when I get up to sitting, I realize it's almost empty, that everyone is outside, shouting and shrieking. The Mothers are shouting too.

Cass's eyes are wide, she's searching my face. "What did you do?" she whispers urgently.

I just look at her.

"You better get dressed," she says, throwing my dress toward me. I yank it over my head and follow Cass, and we make our way out of the bunkhouse into the startling light. The noise is confusing. Cass looks at me anxiously as we start pushing our way through the throng. There are hundreds of girls out here, some laughing, some shouting.

"Enough! Get inside!"

A few of the Mothers are trying to drive the girls back toward the bunkhouses, but to my surprise, no one is taking any notice. We move toward the fence, which is three or four deep with girls, each one bobbing their head to take a look, their fingers hung in the holes in the netting. Cass and I are crushed together in the throng, and around us, there's a growing irritation that some of the girls in front are taking too long.

"Let us see!" come the shouts. "Get out of the way!"

Eventually the girls in the front are pushed aside and as the crowd starts to disperse, I can see it, the wall. The painting. The open door in brown. A triangle of light leading the viewer through the door and beyond the wall into a world of plants and vines and flowers, and the daylight is bringing an element I couldn't have predicted, the shadow of the sun making it leap off the wall somehow. I can't breathe as Cass grabs my hand. I didn't know it was possible to feel so strong and so weak at the same time. I turn to watch Cass take it in.

"It looks like freedom," she whispers, devastated.

I look around and watch, fascinated as the other girls stare, captivated, their eyes on fire. Suddenly I want to cry because I know they have felt something, that something inside of me has spoken with something inside of them.

I look back at Cass, and then we hear a gunshot. We both duck, instinctively, involuntarily. The tension already in our bodies snapping. She grabs my hands in fear, and we cower, our heads down.

"Get in line!" the guards shout, and more come running.

There's a fizzing, dangerous energy now as the Mothers order us to line up, and I suddenly feel in the depths of my stomach how dangerous this is. I've never heard such a noise, excitement, an edge of rebelliousness. It takes much longer than usual to line up, the girls' chaotic energy almost out of control, and after we finally stand together, the Mothers ask us all to put out our hands, and I knew that this would happen, and behind them, I see the guards enter the bunkhouses. The noise of bunks being overturned, mattresses being thrown. I knew this would happen, had buried the empty tubes farther along the wall, washed the brush, and made sure there was no trace of paint left behind on it.

Mother Clement's face is lined with fury, her jaw and throat clenched.

"Put your hands out I said!" she screeches, her voice breaking in anger. I have never seen so much emotion in her expression.

The girls all look at one another and offer up their palms. I watch as Mother Clement begins to walk the line, looking presumably for traces of paint on our hands, our dresses, our hair. She comes closer, her eyes darting everywhere. I hear some of the smallest girls in the other lines crying. I see her shadow shortening on the dirt in front of me and to my horror I feel a little tremor in my hands, not from fear, but from adrenaline. From this feeling, this feeling of taking something back.

Her footsteps get closer, and I try to steady my hands. Her eyes are all over us, and suddenly she's there, in front of me. She stops, not even trying to hide her mistrust, and she studies my hands, narrows her eyes.

"Turn them over," she says, her voice vibrating tightly in her throat. There's nothing there, I know there isn't, but something inside of me knows there *could* be.

"I said turn them over," she says again, her voice pulled thin and dangerous. I concentrate on my hands, try to control the quivering in my fingers, and the best way I can do it is to look her straight in the eyes and slowly show her my palms. She looks back at me, juts out her jaw, lingers a moment before walking on.

The Food Hall is alight with chatter. I don't know if it's my imagination, but it's almost like there's a boldness in how some of the girls are walking. Moving. Everyone is eating quickly in order to go outside again. They have to get us to work today; they want to keep us away from the wall, and the blossoms won't wait.

Deva comes to join us, her face animated. "Did you see it?" she asks.

Cass nods. "It's incredible," she says. I carry on eating, trying not to show too much emotion.

"I felt like I could just step through, step through that stupid wall. . . . Can you imagine?"

I look up. "I know," I say. Deva's eyes are seeing things, I can see it.

"Just stepping through, away from here and those flowers, that green space . . ."

It's then I notice that her eyes have darkened, her voice thick with tears. It's like something's tipped inside of her. Cass grabs her hand as Deva pushes away the tears.

"It made me feel free, that's all."

I smile at her sadly, try to finish my food. Afterward we follow everyone out toward the trucks and there's shouting and booing as the girls see that they're already scrubbing the painting away. Guards with buckets, long brushes, chemicals. The image smudging. There's a palpable unrest, an unease.

They can rub it out perhaps, but I don't think they'll find it as easy to erase it from the girls' minds. It feels different here. It feels like someone's lit a match.

13.

Cass is quieter than I thought she'd be today. We get on the truck, listen to the other girls talk—it's incessant. We catch snippets of conversations all around us.

"I'd go find my brother," one girl says.

"I'd go and see the sea. I've never seen it."

Cass and I absorb them all as the trucks snake their way west. The girls offering up suggestions one after the other before taking them back with giggles. I study Cass's face, wondering what's bothering her. She closes her eyes before I can ask her and I don't want to disturb her.

I've never felt this feeling before, whatever this feeling is. It's a bit like the way I feel when I wake at night, but it has a direction, the energy has somewhere to go, the thoughts have a destination rather than just turning relentlessly in my head. There's a lightness to the girls' faces, like someone's rubbed a veil of dust away, and there's this clarity. Every time I look around at their smiles, every time I think of the painting, my stomach leaps because they can imagine it. They can see something different.

I look across the emptiness, my hands going to the brush in my apron and my mind going to Eliot, wondering if he could get more paint. My tense stomach feeling the urgency of it. We're not going far today, and as Cass and I file off, I watch that she's in front of me, so no one can trip me up again. We collect a ladder each and walk down the line of trees.

Ruth showed me a painting once of an apple tree that had all the colors of the rainbow in it. It didn't look like an apple tree at all, but it *felt* like one. Its branches were all gnarly and tangled and aged, and it looked like it was ancient and beautiful. The trees here are young, cut to a regimented shape, even they cannot grow how they want to grow. I watch Cass as she looks for a place on the trunk to lean her ladder and I climb my side of the tree, and it's then that I remember. I look across at her; in all the excitement this morning, I'd forgotten. I'd completely forgotten.

"It's your birthday," I blurt out. Cass looks over at me, sudden tears in her eyes. She nods.

"I'm so sorry," I begin.

"It's okay," she says. "It's not something to celebrate."

"Fourteen," I say, and the word hangs between us. "There was so much commotion this morning," I begin.

"It's okay," she says again, her voice thick in her throat. She looks so scared.

"Happy birthday, Cass," I say gently. Ruth said that when she was small, there were parties and balloons and good things to eat, and that people played games.

"Thanks, Jess," Cass says as she starts to brush. Mum used to do something silly on our birthdays, do something different, like the time she found apples for Shey or when she filled my room with a string of paper snowflakes.

"Since it's your birthday, I'll tell you a story if you like?"

Cass doesn't turn her head to look at me, but I can see a smile at the corner of her mouth. She doesn't say anything, and I don't press her.

"What kind of story?" she asks eventually. I smile.

"Well, I can tell you about these people who used to eat the sky, and it tasted like watermelon and meat, but they wasted it, so the sky got angry and tore away from the earth...."

Cass shakes her head.

"How about a story about a flying ship?"

She laughs now. "You're so strange," she mutters.

"Okay, okay," I say. "Do you want to hear about a really huge goose and a grumpy old woman?"

She's laughing now and rolling her eyes.

"Okay, the goose it is...."

"Please, no!" she cries.

I watch her laugh, throw up her hand.

"You'll be celebrating your next birthday somewhere else you know," I say, and suddenly her face gets all serious.

"Don't..."

I shake my head. "No, I mean you'll be somewhere else. Free. I'm sure of it."

"I hope so," she says, and then we're quiet, nothing but the occasional chatter from the other girls on the breeze.

"If you are in the mood to tell me a story, you can tell me my favorite."

It's my turn to roll my eyes. "Not *again*," I cry.

"Yes again," she says, and I spend the rest of the afternoon telling her about the North.

♣ ♣ ♣ ♣

There is more laughter as we eat tonight. More chatter. The guards look tense, unused to the volume but with no real grounds to say anything or punish anyone. Cass and I eat together, and Deva puts double helpings on Cass's tray and whispers, "Happy birthday," and afterward we are ordered inside. Perhaps they are afraid of us gathering by the fence again, even though the painting has been smudged out.

We lie together on the bottom bunk and listen as one of the girls in the next dorm begins singing in a language we don't understand. I think it's Polish.

"What do you think it's about?" whispers Cass. I listen. There's a haunting quality to it.

"I don't know," I say truthfully. "Something half-happy, half-sad."

"Maybe someone's heart was broken?" offers Cass.

"Maybe," I say.

"Or maybe someone got lost and is looking for home?" she says again.

We listen as the song comes to an end, and then another girl begins to sing, fragments of another language, another world long gone.

We lie like this for a long time, the air filling with different feelings and shadows until Mother Clement shouts at everyone to be quiet. Cass kisses my cheek and makes her way up to her own bunk.

I lie awake, my mind on the painting, on the way the girls looked at it, and on the singing.

"Happy birthday, Cass," I whisper, but she's already fast asleep.

14.

Father Renatus is standing on the stage today as we file in. This is a special Assembly, and we can all guess why. He's made a point of being there before us, looking down at us, I suppose it's for effect. His head is tilted to the side and his knuckles are white as he holds on to the sides of the old lectern. There's more noise today, nothing very distinct, just a heightened mood as the girls file into their lines. Then the doors close, the sound echoing as the girls quiet down. There's a pause as he clears his throat.

"I know it was a mistake," he says eventually, his voice pulled tight like a trapeze wire, "whoever painted that mural." His eyes scan us.

I keep my head straight, my shoulder touching Cass's.

"And even though the person might not know it was a mistake, they will come to realize it. Whoever did this is sadly misleading you." He's trying to put out the fire in the only way he knows how.

"Whoever did this was saying that you are trapped, when in fact we are a family. A unit."

Charmian is standing in front of us, I see her body

stiffen a little. It's amazing how his voice sounds so modulated, so reasonable.

"We are here to keep you safe from the world. . . ." He wears a pained expression now. "From starvation, from the fighting, from men who would . . ." He stops midsentence. "Opening the door to the outside is a dangerous notion. There is freedom here. Freedom to live and work safely, to be free from hunger, to have productive lives. To make a difference."

Even though no one says a word, frustratingly I can feel the sense of rebellion dissipating in the girls around me, the doubt setting in. This is what I was afraid of.

"Whoever this person is wants to lead you into danger and uncertainty. You, girls, young women, who are among the most vulnerable people in our community."

I can feel the mood flattening further.

"The worst thing, perhaps, is that this person obviously cannot see how much we value them. . . ."

My cheeks are burning now, an anger inside that I know he's trying to reveal.

"So I want you to keep an eye out, so we can identify the person responsible for this, and when we have done that, we can help them. And if we cannot help them, then we will make sure that they are not in a position to unsettle the rest of you again. That they do not think that they can bend the rules at their whim, when all of you are so dutiful, when all of you are such good girls."

He changes tack now, asks us to say the pledge, begins the announcements. Statistics as to how many acres have been pollinated, clawing his way back in control, reminding the girls of their duties, turning their minds inward once again. I tune out as I look at the girls around us. Each one, their eyes seemingly glazing over once again. The goods that we will produce will be exchanged for fuel, arms, batteries, chemicals, irrigation supplies, and my mind shuts it all out. He's poured water with words all over us, and you can feel the tiny flame start to sputter, and my mind turns to Dad.

Mum didn't have to brush. She was too old to be sent there when the first camps were set up, unmarried. She said that she'd never wanted children until she met my father and got to know him. He'd run away from the army, and they met at a protest. They were both standing on the street chanting when the military came, and they had to run. They took shelter in a burned-out car together, hunkered in the back until the soldiers passed. She said they'd been talking in whispers almost the whole time they were in the car together. They were both covered in soot by the time they got out and they were laughing, though she couldn't remember why. Mum said they hung on to each other, were able to bring out joy within each other.

Dad thought speeches, protests, words could change things, but the regime twisted them. He was sure that language was the only way to win, to communicate to people exactly what was going on, to stop them taking the girls and boys, to stop them, but they labeled anyone who spoke out against them as crazy. They took ink and words and smudged everything. Mum said he started self-destructing after Shey and I were born, that he got angry and reckless with the guilt of bringing us into this world, his hope for a better future clashing with the reality, and he would disappear for days and was eventually found and arrested by the militia. I think she really wanted me to know that he wasn't a bad man.

The latest batch of girls are having their hair cut now, one of them is trying not to cry, and I feel suddenly sick when I realize it is Grace Coleman, her head jerking as the scissors cut through her beautiful hair. I feel Cass shrink by my side, and Deva, the other side of her, holds her hand.

My eyes are on Father Renatus. He's watching Grace fighting back her tears and there's something in his face. An ease, a sense of control, and the reason I recognize it is because now I've had a taste of it too.

15.

The trucks are lined up once again and Cass is walking in front of me when I feel a touch on my arm. I shade my eyes and turn, it's Zuri. She's out of breath.

"You're needed with the brushes today," she says. I look at Cass, who's stopped walking and is looking at Zuri too. Her eyes are sunken, dark patches beneath them.

"Grace has gone...."

"Of course," I say.

Cass frowns. "Does that mean you'll be there permanently?" she asks.

I look back at Zuri. She shrugs. "Come on, they're waiting for us," she says as she walks away.

I look at Cass, try to give her a comforting smile. "I'll see you later," I say.

Cass nods, gives me a smile before making her way onto the nearest truck. I turn and follow Zuri back toward the bunkhouse, a strange tugging in my stomach, thinking of those small moments with Cass while we brushed. Those seconds when we'd lose ourselves, forget where we were, and I'd catch a glimpse of her through the blossoms.

Although illusions, they were fleeting moments of freedom.

My eyes try to adjust to the darkness of the bunkhouse once again, and I follow in line as Mother Clement takes us to the Brush House, the feeling of missing Cass complicated slightly by the chance that I might see Eliot and be able to ask him what the guards have been saying about the painting. We wait outside to be let in, and the smell of the chemical glue catches in our throats as we enter.

I narrow my eyes, look around, and see the older guard, another Mother, no Eliot. I feel my stomach sink a little and I walk to where Grace worked, and her station is there as if she had never left. I start to pick up some handles, dipping them into their first coating of glue as my thoughts turn once again to my own painting set.

My brushes were made of hog hair, that's what Mum said, sealed with beeswax and bound together. They were designed so that the paint strokes were even, beautiful, so that they laid down color and saturated the paper with pigment. I lay down the brush handles and line them up one after another. There's no sound except that of the girls stripping back the handles with knives and the thin wooden shavings falling to the ground. The knives here are counted out and in every night, and my mind goes to Eliot once again.

As everything collapsed, they made more and more chemicals, they tried to replace things, do things another way, find new materials. They put money into sciences, not realizing that there is no place for science without a functioning world. At one point, before all the wars and the chaos, they might've made drones or machines or something to pollinate, but once it became a free-for-all, it was like we went backward. Countries that could mine raw materials for batteries kept them to themselves or only bartered with countries that had something they needed, corruption was rife, metals needed for technology became impossible to get, so only the military and the powerful could get phones, keep communications. Governments collapsed, militias took over and ran whatever was left of the countries in the way they saw fit. Sons of those running the army became local leaders. Cass said that Father Renatus was one of General Porter's sons.

They tried to find more and more elaborate ways of doing things. Energy, textiles, food. I can't help but smile at the absurdity of it. Nature gave us wood, it gave us hog hair and horsehair and a beeswax candle, which gave us pure clean light to work by, and yet here I am making brushes like this.

"You're getting good." It's Zuri. She's watching my hands as I dip the snatches of hair into the glue, roll the handle across them, beginning to understand instinctively what to do. I shrug. She's binding the brushes next to me, her eyes concentrating.

"I know what it's like you know," she says quietly, her eyes flicking to the healing skin on my cheek. I look up, frowning.

"The name-calling, the pushing."

I look down again, not knowing what to say.

"My hair. The way they throw hair like mine in the trash bin." I listen to her. She's thoughtful, sharp.

"I heard you can read," she says, and I feel a sudden

warmth toward her. "My grandmother taught me too," she confides. "History mostly, but she loved fiction too."

I startle as the guard gets up, thinking he's coming over, but he walks to speak to Mother Clement, and my shoulders drop in relief.

"Charmian told me once that I was lying, that this has never happened before, that people have never been held like this, made to work like this. She was so stupidly confident."

I can see how much that hurt Zuri.

"The thing is, though, that I'm glad about my hair. My DNA is rebelling against these stupid brushes. My whole body is fighting this."

I smile at her.

"Get back to work!" It's the guard now, he's turned and is looking toward us. We both look down, keep our hands busy.

When I get back, Deva and Cass are sitting on Cass's bunk together. I sit below them and listen as they laugh. It's nice to hear them, that joy. The more time they spend together, the more in tune they are. I'm not angry, not jealous. Sometimes I even wonder whether I'm good for Cass; she needs reassurance, and I can only give her agitation.

After a while I get up and walk outside. There's half an hour before the bell sounds for bedtime. I walk across to my favorite spot, not looking over at the wall where the ghost of my picture still lingers in a white smudge on the concrete. I sit down, my back against the fence, and look at the girls, their minds turned back to bartering.

And then I hear Eliot's voice. "It was brilliant."

I try not to visibly startle, feel my shoulders drop with relief. I sit in silence, listening to the girls chatter in the distance. I pull my knees up, rest my elbows on them.

"I thought you might be angry," I say.

"Why?"

I shrug. "I could've got us both into trouble. I didn't *think* you'd mind but I don't know you, not really."

"You did more with those paints than I could have imagined," he says softly. "And they're worried, really worried."

"Who?"

"The guards, the Mothers, Father Renatus." I find my shoulders broadening a little.

"They don't get worried for nothing. They made us come to a meeting. They've talked about ways to settle the girls down. They warned us to keep an eye out. It's like you've hit upon something they can't control. . . ."

"But they did . . . Father Renatus talked them down—"

"*This* time," he interjects.

"I'm not sure the other girls are ready. It was like something woke up in them but I don't know how to keep it going." My voice chokes in my throat.

"The rioting in the city is worse than ever, the militia is barely keeping control. You can't stop now!"

"Where did you get it? The paint, I mean," I ask finally.

"We get one day a week in the city," Eliot says, "on checkpoints. There's an old factory nearby, ransacked, everything worth anything has already been taken. Except there's paint, artist's paint. They used to make it in the factory. But

I suppose because it's not paint for houses or furniture, nobody wants it."

I think about that for a moment. "How much is there?" I ask.

"A whole room full."

I can feel my heartbeat now; I can't even imagine that much paint. "Is it dangerous to get hold of it?" I ask.

"Yes."

"I didn't realize. . . . I'm so sorry," I say. "I can't ask you to—"

"So you're thinking about painting something else?" he says, an urgency to his voice. "I was thinking I could bring some to the Brush House. Hide it there."

"I don't know, Eliot. It'll be so much harder now. They'll be watching . . . and if they catch us . . ." I can't finish the sentence.

"They can't kill me," he says simply. "I'm not even sure I'm alive."

I smile sadly.

"But if they don't catch us, maybe you could bring this place to its knees."

I feel the weight of his words for a moment, both of us deep in thought.

"There's nothing much to know about me, really," he says eventually.

I frown. "I don't know what you mean."

"You said you didn't know me."

I smile. "Well, I know you obviously don't mind taking risks."

"I only take risks for the important things," he says steadily, "and this is important, Jess."

There's a pause now and I listen to him breathing.

"So? What do you say?"

My thoughts are suddenly loud in my head.

"If we do this," I say, "I'm going to need more brushes...."

16.

It has been a long week of brushing. Every morning, I look for Zuri so I can make the brushes, but she doesn't come to get me. Every morning the guards shout about how much work we've got to do, how many zones need pollinating before the end of the week. They've had us out early all week and keep us late to try to catch up after the storm. I stand on the ladder, my throat dry, brushing with a girl I don't really know. We're brushing gold pollen from one white star-shaped flower to another. I think they're lemon trees.

Cass was dreaming last night, her breathing becoming ragged. It's like she swallows down all her panic in the day so that she looks quite serene, but it sneaks out of her in her sleep when she has less control over it, with the strange breathing, and the tensing of her body, and the way she grinds her teeth. Sometimes I reach up, place my hand on her arm, try to stir her out of it a little, but she was too tense last night.

Shey used to sleepwalk, I haven't thought about it in a long time, but I remember he used to get up sometimes, start walking around the house, and he'd be wailing. I'd startle awake, Mum too, with this panic washing over me, and I'd start shaking from the shock of it before realizing it was only Shey. It was only Shey standing in the kitchen, crying and screaming, and even though I knew it was him, I had to cover my ears because it was excruciating, and it used to astonish me that he never woke himself up. Even with all that noise, he'd go back to bed eventually and in the morning, he'd have no memory of it.

Mum said there were certain noises that had an effect on humans. She said it was like when babies cried, they didn't just affect your hearing, or your nerves, they affected something deep inside of us, connected to something bigger, and that proper screaming and wailing was the same. I believe her, that it's that impulse to pick up that crying child, to throw our arms around the grieving, that makes us human.

The thing is, Shey cried. He cried when they caught him, and I couldn't go to him and put my arms around him. I can't quite picture it because every time my heart starts to put the picture together, my mind shatters it. That sound he made when they were dragging him away, it wasn't words, it was this something from deep inside of him. Something like anger, humiliation, frustration, and worst of all, surrender. They had him, he knew it, and they would make him fight.

I look up and see the guards standing in a line a hundred yards apart, the distance their bullets can travel.

Mum had told Shey what they would do, she wanted him to be prepared. It would start with shaving his head and talking to him about those people who would see him starve and rejoice in it. They would whisper things about the way that the other men would come in over the border and take everything they had, and how they'd take all the women and girls. This was life and death, good versus evil, and she said that it would take a strong mind to be able to overcome the onslaught.

I keep brushing, looking over sometimes at the girl on the other side of the tree, neither of us feeling like talking. Then Mum said the cruelty would start, to harden them up. Perhaps the beating up of someone until they were scarcely alive, the mind games, the brutal language that would petrify them so that each one would be barely human, but most definitely a man.

Eliot said he'd get more paint but that it would depend on when he'd next be stationed in the city. I will need bigger brushes this time and it will be harder, as the guards will be watching more. What we need is to make the brushes and stow them in the Brush House. If Eliot can get the paint there, we can keep it until we're ready, and then, on the night of the painting, he can bury them by the fence. The soil is so dry, it wouldn't take long to dig them up.

I feel a kind of tightness in my stomach at the thought of it, my mind turning back to Shey. It would be his softness that would kill him or keep him alive, I know that for a fact. He would either break his heart like our father did, or his softness would be his strength. This is the thought I cling to, that he is kindhearted to the point that even if they hardened him up tenfold, there would be enough left to save him.

I keep brushing, but it's so hot, so horribly, tortuously hot.

"You're friends with Cass." The girl's voice breaks my

train of thought. I look over, carry on working. She doesn't catch my eye.

"Yes," I say. She nods, a look on her face that suggests something more. I wait, but nothing comes.

"Is there something wrong?" I ask. She looks at me now, and I realize how small she is. A narrow, pointed face. Birdlike.

"I hate people talking, the girls they talk and talk, gossip. I don't like it."

I frown at her. There's a breeze now blowing the wispy bits of hair around her face. "You don't like it?"

She looks pained. "I don't like telling tales."

"What's your name?"

"Emily," she says. Everything she says is considered.

"Emily, what's wrong?" I ask.

"You're her friend, that's why I'm—"

"That's why you're what?!"

She pulls down her arm, stops brushing for a moment. Hangs on to the top of the ladder with two hands.

"They're saying that Deva and Cass are more than friends, that they're together. . . ."

I try not to let anything show on my face. I try to take it in. "Don't be stupid," I say reflexively, defensively.

She looks at me steadily without blinking. "I just heard it, that's all. I thought you should know. It's dangerous." She pauses. "If it was my friend, I'd want to know."

I think of Deva and Cass, the way they laugh together, the way they keep catching each other's eyes. "That's just ridiculous."

Emily shrugs. I consider her. She's often on her own, always at the back of the queue, I've never noticed her being cruel or gossipy. I'm grateful for her forthrightness, her bravery, and the fact that she told me.

"Listen, you're wrong," I find myself saying. "*They're* wrong, whoever said that . . . but thanks for telling me."

She shrugs and carries on working. I carry on brushing too, a strange vibration at my core. I push the pollen from flower to flower, the flecks of gold being disturbed.

17.

It's getting dark, and I eat with Deva and Cass, trying not to look for any signs. What Emily said is ridiculous. I don't say anything, and when they ask me to walk with them to the exercise yard, I go to my bunk to lie down and think. You cannot love someone who's the same sex as you, there's no such thing. There used to be, years ago, Ruth said so. She said that there was a time when people were free to love whomever they wanted to and that one of the first things that happened after they banned the books was to jail people who loved people the same sex as them. People were called selfish, unnatural. Unnatural! After all they did to the world, they called *them* unnatural, but once girls were here just to brush and have babies, it became taboo. It was awful. If there are any rumors, Cass will be taken away, they'll both be taken away.

The girls talk because they're bored, because they need something to think about, I get it, but I don't understand why they talk about one another like that, and I'm too tired, too tired to think about anything. My arms are aching, my knees, the sides of my feet, which press up against the inside edges of the ladder sometimes, and all I can hear is the buzz of the girls in the yard getting louder and louder and then the sound of one of the outer gates that leads out into the camp. The sound of chains, then shrieking. Shrieking like I've never heard before. I sit up, notice how dirty my feet are. I walk to the doorway to see a crowd coming toward the bunkhouse. Charmian is in the middle, her face drawn but triumphant. In her arms is a crate of what look like apples. There's hysteria around her but she walks, queenlike, through the girls as they whoop and scream around her. Another girl follows, a crate in her arms too, and in the distance, I see Cass and Deva turn to watch.

"Get in line!" a guard shouts.

There's general chaos as the girls, in their excitement, can't order themselves. I'm pushed out of the bunkhouse entrance by girls behind me as they rush to the center of the exercise yard.

Charmian has put down the crate, the other girl does the same. Mother Clement blows her whistle, and the crowd quiets.

"Come on," says a girl breathlessly as she pushes past me. I find Deva and Cass and stand beside them.

"This is a treat from Father Renatus," says Mother Clement quietly, forcing the girls to quiet down further to hear her. "It has been a difficult week, and these are a gift to show you how much we appreciate your hard work."

My heart sinks as I hear the squeals of delight. Eliot said they were worried; they must be really worried to send these. A guard picks up a crate and follows Charmian down the line as she gives an apple to each girl, many of whom have never seen one before. I stand around three-quarters of the way down the long line and my stomach churns as I see her from the side of my eye.

"It's to show how valued you are," says Mother Clement.

The first girls are smelling their apples, clutching them to their chests with all their might. Some have even taken a bite, unable to resist, in case someone changes their mind and takes the apples back.

"One for you, and one for you." Charmian's getting nearer.

The little girls can't believe their luck, the older ones are quieter but equally as eager to try the fruit, and my mind goes back to that story Mum told me about the apple that a woman called Eve bit into. How she persuaded Adam to taste it and how the world was destroyed because of her and her weakness. Perhaps some stories are better forgotten.

"One for you, and one for you."

All the girls have raised their hands, their palms open, ready to receive. I can feel Charmian coming nearer and can see that some of the apples are bruised, probably not good enough to barter or trade. My stomach sickens, not because of the bruised apples or the having to stand in line, but because of how patronizing the gesture is, of how gullible Father Renatus thinks we are, and because of how eagerly the girls are playing into his hands. She's three girls away now and I can smell the slightly sour perfume of the over-ripe apples. A small black-haired girl next to me grabs at the fruit and then she's there. Charmian. Standing in front of me, looking at me squarely, a certain pride in her eyes. But I know there is nothing that Father Renatus could give me that I would want.

"One for you, for being a good girl."

I keep my hands by my side and she stops still, in disbelief.

"One for you?" She holds out the apple to me as if she were offering me the greatest of gifts. I look past her shoulder knowing that this could draw attention to me, that the clever thing to do would be to take the apple and throw it away, but I can't. It's like my arms are glued to the sides of my body. And then she looks at me in a way I've never seen her look before. She looks hurt, confused, as if it hadn't occurred to her that refusing was an option, that defiance was a choice.

"Come on!" barks the guard, and Charmian walks past me. And then something remarkable happens. Because I refused, Cass and Deva refuse too. Zuri, Emily, Xiao, Rhiannon. They all refuse. Mother Clement approaches us, ignores the delighted squeals around us.

"There'll be consequences," she says evenly.

None of us react and we wait until she turns to leave, and eventually the apples are taken away and the line breaks up. I notice I've been standing so straight my neck hurts. I feel Cass embrace me for a moment and then she and Deva walk away arm in arm. I start to breathe again, turn around to see the girls eating their apples, their faces in rapture. In the distance Cass looks at Deva with the same expression, and I suddenly realize how blind I have been.

18.

Two days of brushing later, Zuri comes to get me. I get up and follow her. I haven't slept for days, and I've tried not to watch Deva and Cass, but now I've noticed it, I just don't know how many others have too. There's this look that Cass has when Deva is talking, it's like this delight, this bright face, and you know that she cannot control it, and every time I see it in my mind's eye, I think about what will happen to her, to both of them. I think about talking to them, asking them to keep apart, anything to keep them safe, but next to Deva is the only place I've ever seen Cass at ease.

    I follow Zuri across the yard and don't lift my head. When we get into the Brush House, I see Eliot sitting in the corner, but today he doesn't look up. To his right is Emily, being shown how to strip the wood by another girl. She looks up as we come in, gives us the slightest of smiles. I walk over to the tables, and Zuri and I start to work.

    The hardest thing will be to make the brushes so much bigger without anyone noticing and then to place them on the ledge next to Eliot so he can put a cloth over them. At least they won't miss the wood, there is so much of that that a missing piece or three won't register. The girls washing the hair and the ones making the handles will be preoccupied enough, it will be the guard and Zuri that might be a problem. That's who we have to worry about. I decide to leave it until the end of the shift, when everyone gets a little more careless, a little more tired.

We work for a few hours, the stifling heat beading sweat on my forehead. I wind the hair onto the brushes now without thinking, without feeling. These fine brushes are good for pollination, but to paint properly on the scale I am thinking, they'll need to be an inch in circumference.

"It was brave, you know," Zuri says, not lifting her eyes as she talks, "refusing the apple."

I wind the thread, tie it. "I could say the same to you."

She smiles softly. "Just be careful, that's all."

I hear the door open. Mother Clement has left for lunch. We girls only get fed twice a day because we don't work as hard as the Mothers, they say. I glance across and the older guard looks sleepy in the heat. Eliot looks straight ahead. Every hour, Zuri moves down the table and selects and gathers more hair. I wait for her to do so before winding five times the hair into one brush, and I wonder whether the string is long enough, whether the handle will absorb the tension, but it does. I try to work at the same pace, try not to work quicker in panic. Strangely, the bigger brushes take less time, as they're less fiddly. I make sure to tie it off before dropping it into my apron. I pick another handle and sense Zuri coming back, so I drop it once again, carry on as usual. It will have to wait another hour.

By the end of the day, I have four large brushes in my apron, and I know I'll have to get rid of them before walking back to the bunkhouse, as the bulk of them will be visible as I walk. Zuri seems oblivious and I'm sure the older guard is almost sleeping. We have around an hour left and I can see Eliot look over every now and again. He has taken off his jacket and has placed it on the ledge by the side of where he's sitting. I'll have to walk over, ask for water or something, anything, so that I can place the brushes under the jacket. He can hide them when we leave for the day.

I wait, the other girls coming over to look at the day's work, one girl saying she was sure she made more brush handles. I say that it's easy to get confused in the heat. She shrugs, too tired to argue. I turn away as the other girls start to pack up their things for the day, wash their hands.

It's then that I take the chance, move over toward Eliot, who tries to feign surprise at my movements. I stand next to the ledge, turn my body slightly inward.

"I'm so thirsty," I say, trying not to sound too dramatic as to draw attention. He gets up, loops his water flask over his head. As he does so, I slip two brushes under the coat. I wait for him to give me the flask, take a drink, although it is like drinking nothing as the water is lukewarm. I hold the flask with my left hand, try to sneak the other two brushes out of my apron, and as I do, one slips from my grasp and falls to the floor. It's then that I hear a shriek, my throat constricts as I hear Zuri shout behind me. The older guard jumps up and runs toward her, she's spilled hot glue all over the front of her dress.

"Ow! Ow!" she shrieks.

"Get over to the sink!" he shouts, and as everyone's attention is drawn, Eliot snatches the paintbrush in my hand and scoops up the other from the floor, sliding them away under his jacket.

I turn, hurry over to Zuri. The other two girls are taking her apron off over her head. We form a circle of privacy around her so that she can look at the tops of her legs, her forearms. They don't look burnt.

"It's okay, I'm okay," she says.

The older guard and Eliot turn away to preserve her dignity even though there's nothing to see, and Zuri throws down her skirts, laughs a little.

"I can't believe I was so clumsy," she says, looking straight at me. "I'm so sorry," she says again, and I look back at her and I know she knows. I nod my thanks to her and we get ready to go, leaving the spoiled apron and the new paintbrushes behind.

✦ ✦ ✦ ✦

That night, I want to go and check on Zuri, but I can't. She's in a different dorm. I worry that she'll get in trouble for spoiling her apron. I see a hand coming down from the top bunk. It's Cass. She looks for mine and I hold it up, like I did those first few nights, when I didn't know what was going on and Cass knew, so she'd just put down her hand and hold mine.

"You've been quiet," she whispers. "What's wrong?"

I don't answer. I don't know what to tell her. I want to tell her how scared I am for her, about the brushes and about

Eliot and about Zuri, but it's too much, it's just too much. I wait and feel the warmth of her hand in mine. She senses my unease and slinks off her bunk, drops into mine, budges me over. The mattresses are so narrow, hardly wide enough for one, let alone two.

"Tell me," she says in the dark.

I look up at the rungs under her bunk. Say nothing.

"You know I feel that you keep things from me sometimes and I don't know why," she says softly.

I smile. "Couldn't I say the same about you?"

"What do you mean?" she asks.

"Nothing," I say.

"It's like you want to stop me from hurting, but I'm not scared of knowing things. I'm older than you, you know," she reminds me.

"But you're not like me," I say.

"What? Strange?"

I laugh softly, feel the mattress jiggle a little. "I don't know," I say. "You're kind, you think the best of people...."

"I *hope* for the best, there's a big difference."

We go quiet as someone shouts out in their sleep in the distance. Then Cass turns to look at me.

"My . . . my mum died when she was having me. I don't think I told you that," she says quietly. "She lost too much blood. My father was a biological match, they didn't know each other really, and he went back to the army, left me with his old aunt. I hated her. I really hated her," she says, and I can feel the tension in her body against mine.

"She told me I killed my mother."

I wince at the cruelty of it.

"And then I came here, early, as soon as they could get rid of me." She's so quiet now, her voice almost a whisper.

"When I got here I hoped for the best, but some of the girls . . . ," she says, her voice stopping in her throat, "were so cruel. I told myself no one should suffer that; no one should be made to feel so . . . *invisible*."

I think of the day I arrived. The way she stood over me, linked her arm in mine. Held my hand in the night, and it made sense all of a sudden. The way she was with me when I arrived. The way she sat next to me even though my hair was short and set me apart as someone not to be trusted. She knew what it was to be cast away in the world. I feel her head on my shoulder.

"I only know one thing about my mother, and that's that she liked the color blue, so I look for it—in the sky, in people's eyes. Anywhere really. Isn't that stupid?"

"I don't think so."

"It's Deva's favorite color too."

I think about Deva, about the worry in Emily's eyes. "Do you love her, Cass?"

I say the words before I realize I have, afraid that I've betrayed her somehow. That I've had more time to think about this than she has.

She gets up on one elbow, her face close to mine, her eyes darkening. "What?"

"I just want you to be safe," I say, not able to look at her. "I think people have noticed." I imagine it's a feeling like treading on a feather or a flower.

Her face crumples. "I've never had anything of my own," she says, and there's an agony in her voice that I've never heard before and never want to again.

"I'm so sorry," I say. "It's okay. It'll all be okay. Just be careful. Don't be seen together too much. You don't want rumors to spread."

She presses her face into my shoulder now and I listen as she tries to stifle her own sobs.

"It'll be all right," I assure her. "There's always a way out. I promise you, it'll be all right."

I wait for her breathing to slow until, exhausted, she slips into sleep, her breaths lengthening. I try not to move; I don't want to wake her, and all I can think of is the way Eliot says that we could bring this place to its knees, and how we're going to have to if we are all going to survive.

19.

The sheet is whipped from my bed, and I wake with a start. I look through the grayness and see Mother Clement, her lips pursed.

"Get up," she says, her voice clipped.

I stumble to my feet, my hands starting to shake from the lack of food and the shock. She looks at me in disgust. She pulls the sheet off Cass too so that she stirs.

"Get dressed, both of you."

I nod, not knowing what's happening, and force myself awake and try to feel in the dark for my First Dress. Mother Clement wakes Deva, Emily, Xiao, and Rhiannon too, and slowly, even in the dark, it begins to dawn on me that she is waking every girl who refused an apple. We stand by the door, each of us disoriented with sleep. She points at Cass and Emily. "You two for laundry."

They nod and walk to fetch the large bins on wheels that collect everyone's work dresses once a fortnight to be washed. Cleaning the bunkhouse is done every week and is usually shared between everyone. This is our punishment and, as the other girls wake up, our humiliation. It will take hours and hours.

Mother Clement looks at Xiao and Deva next. "You two, sheets," and then she turns her attention to Rhiannon. "You get some buckets. I'll expect all the floors scrubbed, the toilets too."

Rhiannon lingers a moment, unwilling to leave me alone.

"Now!" barks Mother Clement, making Rhiannon jump. I nod at her, and she reluctantly goes to fetch the old metal buckets from the toilets.

There's only Mother Clement and I left now. She studies me as if she's genuinely interested for once. We stand in an uncomfortable silence for what seems like hours.

"Why didn't you take the apple?" she asks, to my surprise. I don't know what to say. My throat is dry.

"I didn't want it," I say, trying to keep my voice steady.

She comes toward me now, her pallid face set against the gray morning. "But why?" she asks again, keeping her eyes locked on mine.

"I don't know," I answer, looking straight past her out to the exercise yard.

She pauses a moment before raising her hand so fast I can't react, and she slaps my cheek. There's no sound except her breathing hard and the shock of my stinging face.

"I asked why, and you will answer," she spits again.

I think about it, I think about what she wants me to say. She's breathing on my face and her breath is sour, she's waiting for me to say something.

"Because I . . . because I . . . wanted there to be

enough for everyone," I lie, staring her straight in the eyes.

She half laughs bitterly, still watching me. "Come with me," she says, her voice quivering with rage.

I follow Mother Clement across the exercise yard and toward the gate. She takes the keys jangling on her belt and opens the gate, stepping aside so I can go through. My heart is beating hard, and I can't believe it as she leads me toward the Mothers' Living Quarters. I follow her to the doorway and a strange sound comes to me, a sound I haven't heard for a long time, the sound of adults laughing. She shoves the door open to a light-colored kitchen area, and the smell hits me immediately. It turns my stomach, makes me gag. It looks like a broken refrigerator has leaked stinking liquid from rotting food all over. I can see it's seeped into crevices and dried in stained patches.

"Clean it up," she says curtly. "All the rotten food needs to go in the bin outside. You'll have to empty it by hand. There are some cloths over there for the floor."

I nod imperceptibly, try not to breathe through my nose, the buzz of flies bouncing along the ceiling.

"After you've done that, you can wash the walls and the crockery."

I look over to where there are dozens of cups. "But they look clean?" I say.

"They'll need washing again," she says, a strange softness around her mouth that looks almost like a smile. "And when you've done that, you can clean the sink."

It's impossible to do it all in a day. She knows this and I know it.

She moves toward a doorway, about to disappear farther into the Mothers' Quarters. I snatch a glance at a clean room with a table, lots of chairs, and she turns around and glares at me as she shuts the door. I turn to look at the floor. The sickening smell, the rancidness of the liquid, a heat rising in my throat. I walk to the refrigerator, prize the door open, and more black liquid leaks out. I feel myself retch, run to the doorway, and vomit outside. I try to steady my breathing, disassociate myself, breathe heavily through my mouth, and then I look up to see Charmian by the gate of the exercise yard, Mother Jackson by her side. A kind of truck has pulled up outside, and I can see Charmian get in. Mother Jackson closes the door. Charmian looks poised, knowing, and I'm sure she looks in my direction as they drive away.

Mother Clement comes and checks on me every now and again, irritated by my lack of progress. The floor is made of concrete here, so the pits in it are really difficult to clean. My back aches, my fingers ache, my legs ache, and my knees are red, raw from having to kneel. I hear some of the Mothers come and go throughout the day, feel the strangeness of seeing the edges of their lives, wonder what it is to live their lives here, to have come here at ten and stayed. I finish the floor, it's as clean as I can get it, and I leave the door open so that it dries, which it will and quickly in this heat. It's then that the truck comes back, I hear it in the distance and walk to the doorway to watch. It stops farther along the other side of the Assembly Hall where the main offices are. I watch as Charmian gets out, moves toward a doorway and disappears.

I start on the walls, my arm aching, and I can almost taste

how bad I smell. After I finish those, I move to the crockery and start washing. It feels like they've forgotten about me, and there's nothing but a murmur of voices from next door. My stomach is aching for food, and I can smell something delicious, unlike anything I've smelled before. Ruth used to describe food in a way that made your stomach ache, and she didn't do it to be cruel, it was just when she was longing for it herself. There was still fruit for ordinary people when she was young, coffee, this bitter drink, and juice and eggs and milk and meat, and when I listened to her talk about it, I used to wonder how it was possible to yearn for something you've never had, to taste something you can't imagine? But I did, and right now the smell of the food is making my whole body feel depleted. I walk up to the door, press my ear to it. There are muffled voices, and I raise my hand to knock.

My hand lingers in the air until my hunger makes me work up my courage and I tap lightly on the wood with my knuckles. There's no answer. They're talking too loudly. I try the handle, slowly, slowly, and open the door ever so slightly, pressing my eye to the crack, and there they are. In the sliver of bright light, I make them out around the table, eating, and it is like something from a painting. There are grapes, I'm sure they're grapes, and cheese, vegetables. I feel my heart sink, my stomach tighten, and this anger rising in me. They're deep in conversation about something, their faces animated in a way they never are in the bunkhouses. I feel the burning filling every part of me until I remember where I am and I close the door firmly once again. I realize I'm breathing heavily, and I stand rooted to the spot. I turn, look back at the exercise yard, look at the dark figures of the girls milling around after their supper of dried bread. I feel weak, from exhaustion, from tiredness, from sickness. There are footsteps and the door behind me opens once again.

"Are you finished?" It's Mother Clement.

I turn. She closes the door sharply behind her. "Yes."

She looks at the floor, irritated. "All right, then, well, go back, stand at the gate, I'll send a guard to let you through."

I nod and strangely it's like I can't understand what she's saying.

"I said, go back, I'll send a guard."

I frown. She looks the same, the same Mother Clement, but I've seen that she's someone different. I feel my eyes bore into her and I know she can feel it. She leans closer.

"Go away," she says slowly and deliberately.

I nod and smile at her coolly. "Of course, Mother Clement," I say.

I turn and walk out toward the gate. She makes me stand there for what must be a further two hours before she sends a guard to let me in. Everyone is fast asleep by the time I get back. I walk behind the screen to wash before I sleep. There's a little clean water in a bucket and I try to wash myself with it, and as I do, my hands and my body seem to shiver with hunger and tiredness and rage. I find myself burning, burning trying to clean myself, to scrub myself clean of this feeling of knowing the truth, until I hear something or someone behind me.

The door to one of the stalls opens and out comes Charmian, and the anger springs into my arms, my fists, and I could easily go for her, except she doesn't look like Charmian at all. She has the same face, the same eyes, but her countenance is different, softer. The skin on her neck blotchy, her eyes shining with having been crying. We look at each other, both of us angry, before she uncharacteristically turns her head and walks away.

20.

"I've been thinking—you're right," says Cass quietly as she watches me swallow down my breakfast. "I'll talk to Deva, we need to be more careful."

She watches me try to fill myself with porridge and pushes hers toward me too.

"It's okay," I say.

"You didn't eat last night, Jess. I did." She fixes me with a look now and I accept the extra food.

"Where were you?" she asks, and all I can think about is how I lay in bed all night raging. "Cleaning a floor in the Mothers' House."

Cass's eyes widen. "I don't think anyone's ever been there," she says in amazement. "What was it like?"

I turn over the stodgy porridge with my spoon. I look at her and know I can tell her the truth, she told me I can tell her the truth.

"She told me to clean the mess on the floor and it took all day and when I finished I was supposed to clean the walls, the cups, and no one came to fetch me and I didn't know what to do," I say, and now I put down my spoon. "And I was listening and they were all in the next room and there was the smell of food, and I opened the door. . . ."

Cass looks aghast.

"I opened the door and they were eating. They had so much food. Good food, Cass. They had fruit, there was meat, fresh food. And they were laughing like they didn't have a care in the world."

Cass frowns, like she doesn't quite understand the words I'm saying. "But how can that be? I thought we ate the same things. Like a family would. I thought they were doing their best by us," she says, and I know it's always given her comfort to believe what she's always believed, to have faith in the people around us.

"They don't live like us, Cass."

"No . . ." She shakes her head now.

"Cass, I'm sorry, but it's true. They make us work, they barter the fruit, they set their own rules. Father Renatus works with the military, the military is the government. We don't live the same lives, Cass."

"But they said we were a family. . . ."

I can't stop myself from letting out a laugh, and Cass looks annoyed now. "Jess, don't. This . . . this is the only family I've known."

I hadn't thought of how she might need this.

"It's okay for you, Jess, you had a mum, a brother, people who loved you." Her eyes are filling with tears and mine are too.

"I'm sorry," I say. "It's just that you deserve so much more, Cass, and I've been doing so much thinking." I reach out to grab her hand. "Last night I felt so powerless, but then I realized . . . we actually have the upper hand here."

Cass looks at me incredulously, goes to speak.

"No, hear me out, Cass," I say. "Please. They're taking our work, turning it into power, and they keep it for themselves. But if we don't brush, if we don't work . . ."

"Then . . . then the hive collapses?" she whispers.

"Exactly!" I nod.

And there's a strange electricity in the air, a charge between us, as we realize the truth of it all.

"It's just so hard to believe, though, isn't it?" says Cass. "After everything we lost, that they'd behave the same way again? The greed?" She's shaking her head now. "I mean, why would they be that stupid?"

"Why would who be that stupid?" It's Deva, she comes to sit next to us, and Cass unconsciously reaches out to touch her hand before she remembers and takes it back again, making Deva look at her strangely.

"Nothing," she says, and looks at Deva. "I'll tell you later."

And suddenly there's no sound except for the clattering of trays, and I can't think about anything except when Eliot will bring me the paint.

I line up by the trucks and wait for Cass. From the corner of my eye, I can see Charmian. I look across, and although she's a bit paler, she seems to be feeling more herself, that steely look back in her eyes. She looms near, before I see the tip of Cass's red plait. She sees me, pushes back her hat. Her face looks tired. I follow her onto the nearest truck, and we get to sit. We listen as the girls settle down, the monotony stifling. Cass is thoughtful.

"I spoke with Deva," she says eventually, "told her we should stay apart." It's like she can't look me in the eye. I nod, wait a moment.

"It might only have to be for a little while," I offer.

She nods now, and I know that there are also words in her mouth that are springy and tight and she can't begin to speak for fear of letting them out.

"It's just to be safe," I say again.

The trucks pass the perimeter and we travel east toward the city. Through the haze you can see the angled outlines of some of the old buildings in the distance. Cass is quiet, and despite so much happening, so much going on, there's nothing much to be said. We arrive and file off the truck and the guard steps in today and separates us as we walk toward the trees. They do it sometimes, to make sure no one gets too comfortable with their friends. I look up, wonder if Eliot is here, but he's not. I fetch a ladder and begin to climb, and for once, I am paired with Willow Harrison, a friendly freckle-faced girl. There are two rows of trees here, and on the other side is a truckload of younger girls. I watch as one determined little kid who must be about eleven tries to carry a ladder toward her tree. She looks over and I give her a soft smile and I can see how scared she is. She climbs up, her hands grabbing at the rungs, the skirt of the dress too long for her, and I gesture to her to tuck it into the strap of her apron, so she doesn't fall. She nods, does what I say, and we get to work.

We work all day, and it's strange because I can't stop watching the little girl. How hard she's trying, how well she wants to do, and how much she wants to please. She's getting more and more tired, her arms unused to the work, her body battered by the heat. I look over at her, pull a funny face, and she giggles, and I imagine Cass when she first got here. Not even ten, the blisters that must have formed on her hands, the ache in her shoulder as she carried a ladder much too big for her, the look in her eyes that just wanted to please, and I feel sick. Sick to the stomach. I hold on to the ladder for a while to steady myself and Willow looks over in concern. I take a few breaths, look over at her, and nod that I'm okay.

At the end of the day, we walk back toward the truck, and in the distance I see Zuri. I walk faster to catch up with her and she looks over, smiles. She's breathing hard in the heat.

"Are you okay?" I ask.

"Sure," she answers.

"I hope you didn't get in trouble about your apron," I say.

"It was fine," she answers, her voice jolting as she walks.

"I . . . I just wanted to say thank you."

She stops a moment now, takes a breath. "For what?" she asks.

I search her face, maybe I made a mistake. "You know, for when Eliot—"

"I don't know what you're talking about," she says. I don't understand. I was sure she spilled the glue on purpose. I take a step back, feeling irritated by the heat, by my tiredness, by the confusion of it all. I nod.

"Listen, don't worry. I made a mistake. I'm sorry," I say.

I feel myself frown, start to walk away, and then she begins to speak behind me. "There's no need to thank me, because I would've done it ten times over."

I turn and she's smiling at me. I stop in my tracks, and she starts walking toward me.

"You're quite the artist," she says as she walks past me. "I'm loving your work. Let me know if you need any help."

I watch as she heads for the truck, a certain confidence in her stride, and suddenly I feel less alone.

21.

We're north again today, and for the first time in a long time Cass and I are brushing together. It's as good a day as it gets here, not too hot, no wind.

Cass has been moping for days. She's eating even less than usual, and when she lies on the bed in the evening in her vest, you can see her hip bones jut out. Every night she keeps her eyes on her tray as Deva puts the food on it and the strange thing is that the way they are together is even more noticeable now they're trying to keep apart. It's like this energy force goes around the both of them and their efforts to ignore each other seem to be so noisy, so obvious.

"Tell me something," Cass says, trying to keep her concentration on the flowers, on anything except Deva.

I keep on brushing. Start to think. "What kind of thing?"

She shrugs. "A story?"

I think of all the books in Ruth's house. How they seemed more of a jumble than a collection, like they were the only ones that survived. She said that the most "difficult" books were burned for fuel first, ones that challenged, ones that upset people, so what was left was mostly the older books, the ones that had less bite to them—what they used to call the classics.

"Tell me your favorite story," Cass says. I feel myself exhale. "Really?"

It's strange, but the longer we're here, the further away stories seem to be. They feel faded in my mind. Perhaps it's the routine, the backbreaking work that leaves your body and your mind so tired, or maybe it's something else.

"Jess?"

I think, think, and all I can see is a little boy on a planet. "There was a pilot who crashed in a desert one time."

Cass looks serious now. "Was he okay?"

"Yes," I say as I keep brushing, "but he needed to repair his airplane, and as he was doing this, he met a little boy, a little prince."

"In the desert?" I nod.

"On his own?"

"It's a story...."

"Go on," she says.

"Anyway, the little prince asks him to draw him a sheep... and he does, and the two become friends. The boy explains to the pilot that he's from another planet and that on that planet a rose grew, and he had fallen in love with it."

Cass frowns. Stops brushing. "Well, that's lovely," she says unexpectedly.

"But the rose is vain and needy, and eventually, even though he loves it, he decided to venture out into the world to find the meaning of love and life."

Cass starts brushing again, but slowly, her mind on the story.

"So he visits different planets and finds grown-ups of all sorts, a king who demands obedience even though he has no one to rule over, a businessman who believes he owns all the stars. . . ."

Cass laughs at this and I'm glad to see her face light up.

"And a geographer who knows nothing about his own planet because he will only be told by others what to think."

I try to bring the story back to mind, that tattered book that Ruth gave me with the names in other languages on the front.

"And?" asks Cass.

"Anyway, eventually he comes to Earth and meets a snake that says that he can return him home if he lets him bite him."

"No!"

"And a flower that tells him that people have no roots."

Cass clears her throat in the warm wind. "So what does he do?"

"Well, he leads the pilot to a well so they can drink, and then he lets the snake bite him."

Cass places her hand on her chest. She's searching my face now. "And did he make it home?"

I look at her. Think whether I should lie or not. "Yes," I say truthfully, without telling her how.

"I don't understand," she says. "Why did he leave home? When he had a place and a love and somewhere to belong to?"

My arm is aching now, so I drop it, shake my hand a little. "Maybe he was curious?"

"That doesn't makes sense," she says.

"Maybe he can imagine something more?"

"But to leave everything behind?" she asks.

"Before he leaves Earth, though, he meets a fox who tells him that they will bring great joy to each other."

"A fox?"

"It was like a kind of cross between a dog and cat, red fur and a bushy tail with a white tip."

"Sounds funny," she says.

"Anyway, he and the fox become friends, and the fox tells him that the only thing you can see with is your heart and not your eyes."

Cass looks up, stunned at that, her forehead crinkling into a frown, and then she nods, her face suddenly serious, and I can tell that she wants to cry.

Cass goes to bed early; she gets tired more easily these days. I eat with Deva and Zuri, and I feel this unbearable tension thinking about Cass on her bunk, thinking about the Mothers' Quarters, thinking about the young girls brushing and how scared I am of my stories fading. I get up, tell the others I'm going for a walk.

The wind has picked up tonight. There are thick clouds, no moon, no stars, just the dead weight of the sky above. There aren't many girls outside either as the dirt is getting blown about. I don't care, I walk to my usual spot, scan the fence quickly for Eliot, and even though he's not there, I sit down.

I look through the darkness toward the wire fence and the wall beyond, and my mind is filled with images, one after the other, my fingers aching for a paintbrush, *my* paintbrushes in the Brush House, and when I close my eyes, I can hear the bristles coat the wall with paint, I can feel the intensity of the color, my tastebuds and my nose filled with the oily, bitter scent of paint. The images forming and disappearing and then forming again.

Mum found me some chalk once, smudgy colors that dried the skin on your fingers, and I loved them, and I liked pencils of course, but you could not beat paint. The thickness of it, the way it ran like honey, the body it had, the presence.

"I thought I'd never see you again."

My eyes snap open with the shock of hearing his voice. "Eliot!"

"Shsh," he whispers.

I have so many questions, so many questions. "Where have you been? It's been weeks!"

He clears his throat. I can sense the hesitancy in his voice.

"Things are"—I can hear him trying to feel for a word—"deteriorating even more . . . in the city."

"What do you mean?"

"There's less food coming in. There've been some people that have starved, others are panicking, there have been attacks on the military bases, there's so much frustration. We've been trying to keep order, but people . . ." He stops, and I feel my heart starting to beat faster.

"People are desperate. I don't know how long the status quo can last. People have had enough; it's been too hard for too long, and they're standing up for themselves more. Protesting."

There's a silence now that's filled with shadows.

"But anyway, I've got some," he says, "paint, that is."

My hearing sharpens, not wanting to miss a thing. "How much?"

"Four big tubes so far. I've hidden it in the Brush House."

"Did anyone see you take it?"

"No. There was so much chaos one day, fighting, these men throwing stones at us in the city and in the middle of it . . ." But he goes quiet. Deadly quiet.

"Eliot? Are you okay?"

"In the middle of it the guard next to me got hit in the head—in his temple—and he just dropped like that. . . ." It's like the rhythm of his words have changed.

"I'm so sorry," I say.

"He wasn't a friend or anything. . . ."

"Does that matter?" I ask, and we let the silence grow around us a little.

"And then the other guard just shot the guy throwing the rocks, and then he was gone too. . . ."

I feel sick.

"It's just that I hadn't seen anything like that . . . not so close. Their faces just changed, and they were gone."

I listen to Eliot, let him feel the words around us in the heavy sky.

"You know, my mum always said that she was sure there was another place."

"Another place?"

"She believes, she thinks, that there's a colony up north, in a hidden valley somewhere." I can almost hear him picturing it in his mind. I smile at the thought of it despite myself.

"Somewhere untouched. Green. Quiet. Where you can

sit under the trees in the shade. Listen to birds. Feel the grass under you."

We're both there in our minds, I can feel it. Him with his back to the fence, looking out at the desert beyond, me looking across at the bunkhouses as the girls get ready to sleep behind the bars. I hear him sniff and I realize that he's crying. There's no way to put my arm around him or comfort him. I wait until he's done, something awful tugging at my heart.

"I'm back in the city next week," he says eventually. "I'll get the rest of the paint. Then you can choose your night."

I feel these pins and needles start at my core and radiate out across my body.

"I'll bury everything by the wall, the brushes too. I'll let you know when it's done."

"Thank you."

I can hear the smile in his voice. "It's okay." He starts to move away.

"Eliot?"

He stops.

"Be careful, won't you?"

"I will"

"No, I mean it," I say. "Please be careful. I don't have many friends. You have to promise."

There's a pause.

"I promise."

22.

I dreamed of the little prince last night, how he fell in love with the flower, and when I awoke, Cass was pulling at my arm, trying to wake me. I line up to wash, tired, thinking about how easy and how difficult the rose was to love and how confusing it must have been for the little boy. Cass is behind me, leaning her head on my shoulder blade, and then I slip behind the screen, take as long as I can to wash and then join Cass in walking to the Food Hall. I feel her tense up when she sees Deva from the corner of her eye, and I have to nudge her to remind her to put up her tray.

She keeps her eyes down studiously and I see Deva do the same. I watch as Cass offers her plate to Deva, neither looking at the other, and then something in Deva's face changes, and her eyes roll back and the old metal spoon she's holding drops from her grasp and clatters on the trays in front of us and she drops to the floor. Cass's eyes snap upward and she looks on in horror as Deva disappears.

"Deva? Deva!" Cass shouts. She abandons her tray, runs around the counter, and I race after her. Deva is on the floor, her body convulsing, her back arched. "Deva!" cries Cass as she kneels down by her side.

I know Deva has warned her about what happens when she has a fit, but seeing it is a different matter. Cass is holding her head as Deva told her to in case she hurts herself, and I become aware of the people around us.

"Help her!" I say, but they just pick up the spoon, look at me with these bored eyes as if they've seen it all before, and there's this hush that comes over the hall as a guard makes his way over. He's behind us now.

"Leave her alone!" he orders, eyeballing Cass, and my heart is beating erratically as I see Cass panic, her face lit up with this kind of agony, and she's whispering to Deva, "I'm here, I'm here," over and over and pressing her cheek to Deva's.

"I said leave her alone! Get up!" the guard orders again, and snatches at Cass's arm. She shrugs him off. My eyes flit between them, and I can see his agitation growing.

"Cass?" I say softly.

But I see she isn't even really aware of his presence—she is fully with Deva. And then the guard grabs her by the arm until she screams, drags her back to the middle of the Food Hall and throws her across the floor.

"Cass!" I check that Deva is coming around and run to Cass, who has landed heavily by a table. She gets straight up and I can see that she's furious and the guard is coming toward us again. "Cass, listen to me. Deva is fine, she's coming around."

It's like she can't even hear me, and she starts moving

toward Deva again. I turn my back to her, try to keep her behind me as the guard comes toward us.

"They're friends, she's just worried," I try to explain, conscious of everyone watching now, but then he shoves me out of the way and my heart leaps as I see him pulling the gun over his head.

"Stay back!" he shouts, and then he hits Cass across the face with the back of his hand. Cass looks shocked, dazed. She looks across at Deva, who's now sitting up, and they're looking at each other, each one in pain, and all I can think about is getting her out of here.

♣ ♣ ♣ ♣

There are huge fires today in the city. Plumes of smoke rising in the sky, smudging out the sun. It's hard to breathe. We travel north again today, and even the guards at the perimeter fence are subdued. I can see Charmian looking at us as she stands in the back of the truck in front. Cass hasn't spoken since we left the Food Hall. I keep telling her that Deva will be fine, but it's like she's tired, she can't keep everything inside anymore. It's almost a kind of recklessness that comes when the pain is worse than the punishment. Being apart from Deva is hurting her.

It's apple trees again today and even the pink freshness of the blossoms can't do anything to raise our spirits. Cass files off sullenly and goes to brush down the line, and to my relief I see Zuri pick up a ladder next to me. She acknowledges me before we walk to the nearest tree and start work.

"Is Cass okay?" she asks.

I nod, try to keep my attention on the flowers.

"Deva and her are good friends," I say, even though I don't know why. I know Zuri will understand. She nods.

"I've been talking to the girls in my dorm, they've had enough," she says quietly, looking over her shoulder to see where the nearest guard is.

"Sometimes I think that too, but then nothing changes," I say.

"It's different this time." She brushes and talks. "Every now and again, someone starts talking about that door, it's like they can't stop thinking about it."

She senses my skepticism. "I can't, anyway. You know I dreamed about it?"

I think about that.

"About pushing it open, about stepping out somewhere else . . ."

I smile at her, but then the smoke gets thicker, and I start to cough, I feel weak. The questions that have been gnawing at me for weeks surfacing.

"But what if . . . what if it leads nowhere?" I ask, finally. "What if Father Renatus's right? What if it's all a false hope and there's nothing better out there? How could I live with that? Leading everyone to something false, to something worse?"

She looks at me as if I'm stupid. "He's got to you," she says, crestfallen.

"No." I shake my head. "It's just that . . ."

"It's just nothing. . . . ," she says sharply. "Jess, what could be worse than this?"

"If we pushed on the door, I worry about the young ones. The young girls."

She stares at me now, her eyes softening with pity. "You're worried about them? Worry about them staying *here*!" The way she says "here" makes me feel sick.

"They brainwashed us! They're not keeping us safe, they're using us. Did the books not teach you anything?"

I feel my face flush, embarrassed.

"*We* are the harvest, Jess. They consume us, and they throw us away." And the intensity in her voice seems to galvanize something inside me.

23.

Cass sits cross-legged on the floor; I watch as she rakes the soil through her fingers. She hasn't said anything for days.

"Eliot's got some more paint," I venture, eager to get some kind of reaction out of her. Her face blanches at this, her body suddenly still.

"When were you going to tell me?"

I shrug. "I didn't want to give you anything else to worry about."

I see Cass's face and I know she's thinking of Deva, of how much she misses her.

"We can't keep living like this, Cass. It's not even living. Zuri, Emily, Deva, they all feel the same . . . and if they do and we do . . . well, there must be more. I hid some brushes, bigger ones this time. If I do another painting, I could test the waters. . . ."

"But what do you think will happen?"

"I don't know exactly. But something? Anything? If we can just open people's eyes . . ."

"Their hearts?" Cass asks quietly.

"Those too. . . . When I've got all the paint, I'll have to choose a night. It's the general's Victory Parade soon."

Cass knows how they try to foster unity in the city every year with a stupid military parade. "But if you're caught?"

I think about this. "What? What if I'm caught? How much worse can it be than this?"

We both sit in silence a moment, my mind going to the chaos outside the camp wall.

"Do you think they thought they had time to work it out?" I ask the night as much as anyone.

"What do you mean?" she answers.

"It's the only way I can make sense of it. They must've thought they had time to work things out even as the world was changing. They must've thought that every step was reversible and if you slowly worked your way backward, you'd get back what you lost."

I listen for an answer as Cass contemplates this. "I don't know," she says.

"It's just strange that they thought they had the power to do that. To understand things that were so complicated. Did they think that they could revive coral or spark life back into a dragonfly? It's so stupid, isn't it?"

"Maybe they hoped for the best," she says quietly.

I smile sadly. "They made the same mistakes over and over again even though they had words and books and ways of speaking to one another all the time."

"You think too much," Cass teases, touching my arm.

It's then that we see a figure approaching. Deva. Cass jumps up, runs toward her, hugs her hard. I look around, it's dark, it should be okay. I can hear them whispering urgently, they have not seen each other since Deva's seizure. They come toward me and sit together, suddenly silent, and even though I know I can stay, I feel I should leave them alone in this dark corner of the yard under the suffocated stars. Just for a moment, just for now.

♣ ♣ ♣ ♣

It's dark. Mother Clement has started sleeping in here since the painting. They've stationed a Mother in every dorm to keep an eye on us. Through the shadows I can see her lolling head. I look up for Cass's hair, for the shape of her back in the bunk above, but she's not there. I frown, listening. I reach up, push up her mattress a little to double check, and I feel a trembling deep down. I look across at the window, the bars, the desert beyond, and it is still, stiller than it has been for weeks. I pull my head from the pillow and look back across the dorm. There's nothing but the light of the moon on the floorboards. I start to time her. Perhaps she went to the bathroom just before I woke up, so she should be back in a few minutes. I count, thinking about when I would count down to Mum coming home. A habit I still have sometimes.

After Shey would wrap his arms around her and beg her to be careful out there, like he would every time she left the house, I would start counting. It would take Mum around thirty-seven minutes to reach the ration queue in the city, two thousand two hundred and twenty seconds in fact. That was how I measured it, around one thousand eight hundred seconds to stand in line, and two thousand two hundred twenty seconds to come back. It seems silly I suppose, when you have all the time in the world, when you could do nothing all day, but the only way to keep sane is to measure your time out like that so that it has some meaning, some value.

Shey used to say that the thing about time was that if you were in a situation for a week or a month, time could be counted down in hours and seconds, but if the situation you're in lasts years, then time becomes irrelevant. It disappears, because it doesn't matter anymore. I think about him now, my mind coming closer to him than it has in weeks. The way I would get on his nerves with my counting, how he would come and hit my arm, press his hand on my mouth sometimes to stop me, but I just couldn't shut up. I couldn't stop. I wonder if I should count until I see him again.

There's a noise. I listen, hear some footsteps, bare feet on the floor. I look up and it's Cass. My shoulders drop in relief. She doesn't know I'm awake as she steps quietly, heel to toe, trying not to wake anyone. She moves to climb to the top bunk, and when I touch her leg, she startles, tries not to yelp. Then she bends down, comes closer to me until her shining face is next to mine. She's exhilarated.

"Where've you been?" I mouth.

She pushes me over, gets in next to me, turns her body to the side, and presses her mouth up to my ear. "What?" she asks almost inaudibly.

"Where've you been?" I can't help but sound a little annoyed. She's cold, it feels like she's been out of bed a long time.

"Nowhere."

She's lying. I know she's lying; she knows she's lying.

I look at her face and there's something different about her. She's glowing for the first time in months. It's like she's switched on, lit from the inside, some life about her. She's looking at me, her eyes huge in the shadows.

"What's wrong? What's happened?"

It's like she's bursting. I can actually hear her quiver. "Cass, you're scaring me," I say.

She's looking at me, her eyes far away. "Cass? Please tell me what happened?"

She searches my face, and I notice for the first time that there are tears running down her cheeks, tracking their way onto my pillow.

"I . . . I kissed her," she says, as if she can't quite believe it herself, and she puts her hands over her mouth. "I kissed her, Jess, and it was like you described. . . ."

It's like she's been stung by something, and I look at her, wondering what it felt like, the brushing of lips.

"I kissed her," she says again in wonder, "and it tasted like apples."

24.

There are more girls than usual on the stage today, and it's so hot, Father Renatus has taken off his jacket and stands there in his shirt, with these patches of sweat discoloring the material under his arms. There must be twenty girls today, and since I've been here longer now, their faces are more familiar. Father Renatus brushes his forehead with the back of his hand, and I realize how white his hands are, how little manual work he must do, then there's a hush as he clears his throat.

"We are here today to celebrate the fact that we are making great progress with brushing." The hall is full, a sea of brown check fabric.

"And to celebrate the impending marriage of these girls."

There's a murmur now as some of the younger girls try to look over to see if they recognize any of them.

"They have done their duty and are ready to move on and provide the world with new hope in the form of children."

Mother Jackson is on the stage, her scissors ready, and the first girl approaches her, sits on the chair, the tips of her toes on the floor and her heels resting on each leg like a child, like the girl that she is. She covers her face with her hands as Mother Jackson gathers up her black hair.

"So let us celebrate and show our thanks." Father Renatus begins to clap, and the guards look at us.

The little girls start clapping first and then the older ones, and as I look forward toward the front of the hall, I see the little girl I pulled a funny face at. She's not clapping, her eyes studying what's going on, as if things are beginning to dawn on her. I feel Cass's elbow in my ribs, and I know that I must clap too and every cell in my body rebels against the idea but then I remember not to draw attention to myself and I raise my hands, clap them together uncertainly, and we watch as girl after girl sits, her hair hacked off, and the clumps falling into the baskets behind and I know that it will be sorted and washed and made into brushes by Zuri and Emily and me and I feel ill.

Father Renatus surveys us, doesn't look over at the girls as they are led away by the guards to collect their belongings from the bunkhouses, not that they have anything of worth. The last girls have left and there is a strange pause as we wait for Father Renatus to resume, or finish up, or do something, and then I notice his fingers gripping the lectern again and I frown.

"The reason," he says slowly, "we celebrate what these girls have achieved is that they are doing their duty. It is vital for us all that each one of us plays our part. That each of us is part of a community. We cannot survive alone."

I look over at Zuri. She's looking at him, a sense of growing dread on her face. I look back.

"And it has come to my attention that some of you do not care in the same way as others. That you do not see yourselves as part of our family."

I can sense Cass's body tensing beside me.

"It gives me no pleasure to remind you that we are vigilant, that we take great care in rooting out those who will not work in the service of others."

There's more noise now, nothing distinct, just the sounds of dread and curiosity.

"And we try to show our appreciation for your work, but for some it seems this is not enough."

My heart begins to hammer, and I scan the heads in front of me for Deva, wondering if they know, if they know about Cass and Deva. . . .

"Yvonne O'Neill?"

At this, there's a commotion, and the girls start to whisper.

"Would you please join me?"

A girl from one of the other bunkhouses breaks her line and begins to walk toward the stage. She has her head down, her hands clasped in front of her.

"Up here, quickly," Father Renatus snaps. She walks up the steps, moves reluctantly toward him. "Now, share a story with us."

The color on her cheeks deepens, and her breathing is rapid. "Come on!" His voice is like sandpaper.

"Someone has come of age, sir. . . ."

He's watching her now, his jaw tense. "Speak up!" he barks.

"Someone has come of age, sir."

There's the sound of murmuring among her friends left

behind in the line. "Silence!" he shouts, his voice echoing around the hall.

"Continue...."

"Someone has come of age, sir, and has been hiding it."

"Louder!"

"Someone"—her voice is forced, it breaks—"has come of age and has been hiding it!" She's crying now.

"And their name?"

There is a deathly hush. "Willow Harrison."

I'm looking at Willow's friends as her name is announced, and Willow looks devastated. Her forehead crinkles, uncomprehending, and she's entirely still as the others jostle around her, and suddenly there are two guards holding her arms, one either side of her.

"Willow Harrison became a woman a few months ago." The euphemism sounds dirty in his mouth.

I've heard of this happening before.

"But she has been concealing this fact."

Willow is shaking her head frantically now, tears in her eyes. Her friend is trying to get to her, get past the guard, but she can't, and they begin to drag her to the front of the hall. They turn her around so that her face is visible.

"This is the face of a traitor," Father Renatus says. "A girl who does not want to do her duty."

Willow looks in shock, her eyes wide, terrified, and I look away. I cannot watch. Cass stares at the floor.

"We try and look after our girls to the best of our abilities, so this is"—he chooses a word—"disappointing."

He pauses a moment, makes sure everyone is listening.

"Once you become a woman, you have womanly responsibilities. You must grow up. If you are old enough to bring forth a child, then you are old enough to cope with the consequences of not facing your obligations."

At this, the guards begin to drag Willow outside and her friends shout in terror. But Willow herself is silent. I close my eyes. The doors slam shut once again and there is nothing now but the wailing of some of the girls and the deathly silence of everyone else.

25.

Ruth had this book; she gave it to me. It was an art book about how to draw the human body. It was old, stupidly old, but I loved it. There were pages of figures, women mostly, all of them nude, posing in different positions. I remember Shey finding it one day and laughing and whooping and teasing me until I got really cross and hid it.

I wind the string around the brush, listen as the other girls work. I tie off the end of the string and grasp another handle.

There seemed to be so many ways to try to draw a person, and they'd sketch a grid on the page and then draw the person into the grid so that you kind of cut up the person into different bits, concentrate on one part at a time until all the parts suddenly made a whole. I tried it, but it was really difficult. You had to be so careful that all your edges lined up, that everything was in proportion, or something would look wrong, and weirdly, it was never obvious what wasn't right, but your eye knew something was off kilter.

I didn't like building the people in the grids, so I tried another way where you'd kind of break down the silhouette of a person into shapes, rounded ones. An oval for the head, and a cylinder for the neck and then the body and you'd build them up on the page almost like a sculptor builds up clay so that a form begins to emerge. I found that better, but it was still strange. To start from a general shape and try to get nearer and nearer to the form you were looking for.

It's quiet today, the girls working. Eliot is not here, and I'm impatient to know if he's getting the rest of the paint.

The book's models were all pretty similar, though—white skin, rounded shapes, no hair between their legs, these long, almost squared fingers. Clean, perfect, their eyes almost always looking away, and these dimples on the tops of their buttocks where they'd carry just the right amount of roundness. They looked alien compared to Mum, to Ruth, to me.

Mum was getting thinner and thinner, the skin on her face mottled with the sun, her hair graying where the parting was. And Ruth, her arms were thin and there'd be this loose skin where her underarms were, but she was so beautiful with her white hair. Just not in the way these women were. And then there was me, my body hard, bony, tense. The edges of my shoulder blades sharp and my serious eyes, as Mum would say. I could not imagine, I cannot imagine being that soft, and what I remember is that in the book they would often be holding roses, the petals falling lightly on their white skin. There was never any blood, or marks, like the scars on my mother's arms, there were no angles, no unevenness, and I wonder what kind of world made those women, or what kind of world wanted to rub half of women out?

My handles are finished, so I walk down the table, wait

for more, trying not to look over to where the paint and the brushes are stored. I tried to draw Shey hundreds of times and each time I got a little closer. He was so fidgety that I preferred to draw him when he wasn't looking, when he was reading or asleep. The proportions were difficult, and the lengths of the limbs, then the light in the room, and then the features, and the nose. The nose was so hard, and then once I'd gotten better at that, the eyes, and what I learned was that you were not really painting what you could see. You were trying to paint what was inside that person. You were painting what was inside them by painting only what you could see, and it really didn't make sense, but then you could draw eyes over and over again, and then suddenly, one day, you'd draw a pair and they'd be looking at you. They would follow you around the room. I take the new handles and walk back to my station, smile at Zuri.

There was a section in the book about these Pre-Raphaelite models with hair like Cass's, each one with haunted eyes and sad expressions, their gaping mouths and their pallid complexions, and I wonder why they were like that. They were so beautiful, so seemingly full of life, and sometimes I would sketch them happy, laughing, their heads thrown back in mirth, or raging and jealous, or irritated and aloof. That's how I sketched Mum too.

It's hard to describe drawing your mother, the person you've come from. It's like seeing yourself and yet seeing something else. The shapes within her that are within you. Her stubborn jaw, her worried forehead, the crinkles around her eyes when she laughs, deeper than yours because she's older, but there's more than that too. I loved drawing her even though she'd get bored with sitting and sitting. Mum sitting on a throne, a scepter in one hand. Mum swimming in the sea, Mum walking through a garden. I tried to give her more lives than she had.

✤ ✤ ✤ ✤

It's the end of the day and the girls are packing up but my mind is still on Mum. She said that a day would come when no one remembered the life before the collapse, when without books, people would forget about stories, there would be a nothingness, and I remember asking her whether that would be easier, a bit like Ruth and her memory. Ruth's memory had been getting a bit fuzzy and it upset her, and the reason that it unsettled her was because she remembered just enough. When the time came when she didn't know whether she remembered or not, and there was only oblivion, maybe her mind would be more restful. Then Mum came toward me, shaking her head, and she held my arms, her face suddenly serious, and made me promise to always, always try to remember.

It's getting near bedtime. I can feel it in my bones. Although I haven't been brushing today, I'm tired, heavy with the smell of the glue in the Brush House, the thinking about what is to come. I sit, looking back at the bunkhouses, and I realize that the moon is low tonight. I can see Cass in the distance talking to someone, and most of the other girls start to make their way inside. I begin to get up, giving up on Eliot, when I hear a voice.

"I've got the rest of it."

I close my eyes in relief.

"I'm sorry it took so long. . . ."

"It's okay," I whisper.

"There's a guard, he's paired with me, watching me all the time. I hate him." Eliot is standing directly behind me.

"I've buried it all already."

"Already?!" I ask in surprise.

"I had an opportunity, and I took it," he says, and I take it all in.

"So, we're ready," I say.

"We're ready," he says.

My stomach starts to tighten, and we both fall into a silence.

"Do you know what you'll paint?" he asks quietly.

I think about this, have been thinking for days about what I will do, but every time I think about it, I change my mind.

"I don't know yet," I say truthfully. "Ideas keep forming, but then they slip away."

He listens. "My dad was like that," he says softly. "He would compose these songs, and to start with he'd just have one chord, or one word, or one note, nothing much. But then a moment would come when he finally felt ready, and he'd start to put it all together, and it would all make sense."

I smile at this.

"You've just got to trust it," he says. "You've just got to trust that it will be there."

There are some guards unlocking the gate to the exercise yard, their keys jangling in the quiet. The gate squeaks open.

"There's a full moon tomorrow night and a practice for the military parade, so a lot of the guards will be out late."

I think about this.

"It would make sense to do it then," he says.

We watch as the guards approach the bunkhouse purposefully. "Tomorrow night it is," I say.

Suddenly there's a commotion, and my eyes are drawn to the squares of light that are the doorways and windows of the bunkhouses. I frown. There's screaming now, and I jump up, my heart starting to flutter. Another scream, and then my blood freezes. It's Cass, I'm certain it's Cass.

"What's going on?" Eliot asks.

"I don't know," I answer, but I instinctively start to run toward the bunkhouse. As I get nearer, I try to make out what's happening and I see them dragging a figure through the doors roughly, one guard each side, the girl kicking and screaming, and after them comes Cass. She's shouting, pleading, wailing, and I can't think, I almost can't see.

"Cass! Cass!" I shout, and somehow she finds my face amid her panic. She turns her head, her eyes locking onto mine. She looks terrified, otherworldly.

"Deva! They're taking Deva!" she screams.

Zuri appears by Cass's side, Emily too, and they take hold of her arms, stop her from chasing them. Deva is screaming, kicking up the dust with her heels, and my heart breaks to see the look on Cass's face and the way the other girls are restraining her for her own safety, trying to reach her with their words.

"Cass, listen. Cass . . . ," says Zuri softly.

"They're taking Deva!" Cass wails again as Deva is dragged farther away, and then there's the sound of the gate opening, the clink of keys, and Deva's cries getting more and more distant.

I stand, helpless, breathing heavily, trying to think. Think. Cass can have children; she's more valuable to them than Deva. I watch, paralyzed, as Zuri pulls Cass close, lets her bury her head in her neck as Emily looks on, distraught. Cass's body crumples in this horrible defeat, and then I look up to see a figure leaning on the doorframe. It's Charmian, her arms crossed, a strange satisfaction on her face.

26.

"Cass? You've got to get up," I say quietly. I stand next to her bunk, rub her cheek with my thumb. Her eyes are swollen from crying, her eyelids all puffy, her skin blotchy and damp. "Cass?"

I know she's awake, hasn't slept, but she won't listen. I decide to leave her, get in the wash line and bring some breakfast back to her. I start to queue, my rag on my shoulder.

"So they're both traitors." It's some of Charmian's friends, and my body stiffens. I'm so tired, so tired of this. I step forward, try to tune their voices out.

"No wonder they're best friends. One of them tried to run away before she even got here and one of them's . . . confused."

I concentrate on breathing, swallow down my words.

"It's good that Deva's gone, though, because now Cass can go back to normal. Get cured."

I close my eyes, try to keep the emotion within the grid of my frame. I couldn't sleep either, kept thinking about what they'd do to Deva. She's not allowed to marry, we know that. My stomach lurches at the thought of it. She's young enough to work, she's got that on her side. I try not to think about what could happen to her, about what could happen to her all alone.

I step forward and move behind the screen. I try to wash, my mind running everywhere, and rub myself dry and start walking past the line of girls. I try not to feel their eyes on me, and then I hear her voice, Charmian, and she's laughing. There are some girls around her and she's saying something about Deva, and I can't not listen.

"Can you imagine walking in on that? Two of them kissing like that, really into it."

I stop walking, close my eyes, a wave of nausea coming over me. My washrag in one hand and the words in Charmian's mouth making what happened sound dirty.

"It's disgusting, both of them getting all hot and sweaty."

The girls are hanging on her every word. I turn unconsciously, walk toward her, and I see her turn and look at me, preparing herself to enjoy the confrontation.

"You make me sick," I say.

She smiles. "What's sick is two girls together, that's what's sick. It's sick and selfish."

"Selfish?"

"They going to have babies, are they?"

The girls all laugh, and I can feel my hand curl into a fist. "Is that all you think about?"

"What do you think we're all here for?" she asks.

"Is that all you think we are? Is that all we deserve?"

She looks confused, plasters on a fake smile, her only currency called into question.

"Is that all you want?" I ask.

Charmian cocks her head now, but I'm just getting started. "Or maybe you're just jealous?" I say. "Is that it? Jealous of two people who actually care about each other? Who actually feel something real?" I can see her smile falter.

She stands for a moment in complete silence before sharply raising her hand to slap me. But this time I grab her wrist. She's shocked. Embarrassed.

"Don't you dare," I say again, my voice quivering dangerously. "Don't you dare."

Her face hardens, inches away from mine. "You're so smart, aren't you?" she says. "But you still can't see what or who is in front of your face."

She jerks away her wrist, tilts her head. "Watch your back, Jess," she says coldly.

♣ ♣ ♣ ♣

I manage to get Cass from her bed. I don't want her to get in trouble. I press some bread into her hands from breakfast and lead her to the trucks. I make sure I'm behind her as we get off in the north, and pick up the ladder by her side. I see Eliot from the corner of my eye, but he doesn't acknowledge me. I tell Cass to climb the ladder and she does so robotically, her hand moving upward as she reaches the top.

We brush in silence for the whole day, my eyes flitting over to Cass every now and again, but she won't speak, she won't look at me, and it's not because she's trying not to, it's because she can't. It is because the world took this precious thing she had and shattered it on the ground. It's because something that was so private was ripped open and shown to everyone and laughed at. I know the best thing I can do is say nothing, just be here, not press her.

My mind goes to Charmian, the knack she has of making you feel off balance, the way she warned me to watch my back. I know enough not to let someone like that get to me, but there was something bothering me, something in her eyes that I hadn't seen there before. It was truthfulness. I think it over, think of what she might have meant. I drag my mind back to the flowers in front of me, try to center my thoughts.

They say we'll be in the greenhouses soon, that the blossom is coming to an end for this year, even though there are no certainties now, but I have noticed that there seem to be fewer flowers, the pollen looking sparser.

I look at Cass, who has stopped brushing. "Cass?"

She looks lost, scared.

"Cass?"

I'm frightened she'll fall off the ladder, so I start climbing down and around the tree and climb up behind her just in case. I can see Eliot approaching.

"Cass?" I whisper in her ear. "You okay?" She nods.

"Does she need water?" It's Eliot. I look down, cup Cass's elbow, and tug at it so that she follows me down the ladder. She slumps to the ground, and Eliot comes over, pulls the flask of water over his head, unscrews it. He passes it to me, and I press it to Cass's lips.

He looks at me, concerned. "I wanted to say that I'll try to find out all I can." At this Cass looks up, her eyes widening.

"I can't promise anything, but I'll try to find out where she went."

I press the water toward Cass, but she pushes it away. "Cass, please," I say sternly, "you *have* to drink, you have to eat. If we're to get out of here, you've got to help us."

She looks from my face back to Eliot's. "You'll find out where she is?" she asks again, her voice broken.

"I'll do my best," he says. "Now drink."

She nods and, without taking her eyes off him, takes a little water before starting to cough. I look up at Eliot and I know that I don't have to tell him how grateful I am.

27.

Cass has fallen asleep before food. I look at her in her bunk and agonize over whether to wake her or not. She is thin, painfully thin, so that her cheekbones are sharpening and the freckled pink plumpness under her eyes has dissolved into dark smudges. In the end I decide to let her rest, hoping that she will eat in the morning.

It's getting dark now, the girls starting to settle down as I lie under Cass's bunk and watch as the last of the girls walk past, their washrags over their shoulders, and I realize that there's something wrong. My body, which usually vibrates with tension, is still, a strange calmness inside me that I've rarely felt before. The only other time I felt like this was when I stood at that border crossing with Shey, jutting out my chin, my eyes steady and challenging. It's like the whole buildup is a storm, and then in its eye, I go quiet, leave myself, find somewhere else inside me that's usually cut off, stubborner, bolder. I feel for my heavy legs, my arms, and they're not shaking, they're relaxed, the muscles soft because for once I have something to do.

That's the thing with living now, there seems to be

nothing to be done above and beyond what must be done to survive. Mum would go to the ration line, collect clothes, try to barter things, come home, and here, we wash, we eat, we brush. There is nothing else.

I wonder what it must've been like to have choices, to be able to do things. To choose to go for a walk, or what to do for work, to have control over your own time. I think it must've been precious. People must've reveled in it, and sometimes I imagine decadent days where I do the same and I'm in my own space and I wake up safe and I eat some fruit. I can't imagine where I live, but I eat the fruit and then I go for a walk, maybe by the sea, or in the woods, or into the city and stop at a café and then maybe I work. I imagine what that would look like, and I think I would do something with the people who used to act things out and that was their job, or maybe I'd be in the background painting the scenery I saw in one of Ruth's books, and then in the evening I might meet some friends and have some food and go home.

Every time I imagine those days, my insides start to tremble at the impossibility of them, and although Ruth described them to me, they feel so far away now. Faded. The images in my mind curled up at the edges like the posters in my room at home. I listen as Mother Clement comes in and takes her seat by the window and begins to stare into the darkness, the set of her mouth tight. Perhaps it is best that those images are fading, but I wonder whether people actually did love it? To live like that. Or if they thought that there was something better? Something shinier? Something more, and in their looking for it, they destroyed what they had. I turn on my side, look out at the window. Cass groans in her sleep.

I think Cass would be a teacher, or one of those people that looked after animals, and I know she would have married for love, and unlike me, I can see her as a mother, red-haired children with rosy cheeks and dirty feet. And Zuri? She would be someone important, sorting things out, running a business of some kind, and Emily, maybe she'd be an architect.

Mum asked me once about what I would be if the world wasn't what it was, and I told her about the painting, about painting the backgrounds, and she said that I would be better onstage, not a supporting act, but I told her that no one can act if the scenery isn't right, and she laughed, told me I was strange and that she loved me.

It's quiet now, the girls have fallen asleep. There's a full moon, just as Eliot said, but the clouds are mitigating it so that it's not too bright, the light coming in opaque and soft. My thoughts turn to the rock Eliot said he'd put on top of the buried paints, and I turn my eyes to see Mother Clement's head start to loll.

I stare up at Cass's bunk, and I let myself think again about the backgrounds I would paint. Forests and castles, skies and animals. I would fill every stage so that the people watching would think that they were somewhere else and that the actors weren't pretending but were real. That would be magic, surely. That I could take the paint and make it come alive and let it breathe reality into the people around.

Mother Clement is snoring now, the pattern of her

breathing has slowed right down. She's in a deep sleep. I get up, my senses sharpened, leave my dress at the bottom of the bed, place the soles of my feet on the floor. My skin prickles with the excitement, and I slowly pull myself to my feet. I stand a moment in my vest, looking around, trying not to breathe so that I can listen to the breathing patterns of everyone else. What I have learned is that it is very difficult to fake being asleep. Then I turn, the skin of my feet sticking a little to the floor, and make my way over to the door. Mother Clement is slouched in the chair, her soft body spilling over the sides of the seat. I hold my breath, try to slide the door open. It's stuck. I push across again; it moves a little, then stops, and I notice to my surprise that it's locked. The metal bar across. My heart starts to pump, and I can see the keys hooked onto Mother Clement's belt. My mouth feels dry. It's too risky. Much too risky, but if not now, then when? There are fewer guards tonight and the paints might get discovered any day; I may not get another opportunity.

I make my way across toward Mother Clement, her head now falling farther down, her arms curved in her lap. The keys are resting on the side of her dress. I can hardly feel my body as I look at them glistening in the darkness. They'll rattle, they'll move in my fingers and wake her. I think, think. The only way to grab them will be to grasp them confidently, not let them rub against one another, which, considering there are around five keys, is easier said than done. I'm right next to her. Her gray skin, her gray hair, and I feel tall by her side, and suddenly I feel sorry for her. For her soft body, for the wear on her skin, and the age on the back of her hands.

I reach out my hand, slowly, slowly, my whole body getting nearer and nearer until I can almost feel the heat of her body on mine. I reach out my fingers, my heart thrumming at how dangerous this is, but I just do it. I grasp them, strongly, unhook them from her belt. She starts and sits up and for a moment I think I might die with shock as she opens her eyes and stares into the darkness, and my heart is in my mouth as she starts to blink once again slowly, slowly, and I realize that she is still asleep, and her head lolls to the other side and I'm standing there looking at her with the keys in my hand.

I turn, my heart painful in my chest, and walk back toward the door, slide in a key, quietly, slowly, only to find it doesn't work. I close my eyes in the darkness, count to three, try another, and to my relief find that it opens the door. I only open it as much as I need to and slide out, closing the door behind me. I look around, I can't see anyone. I can't see a guard, but even though Eliot said there'd be fewer, I know they'd never leave the dorms understaffed for long. I crouch down, leave the keys outside the door.

I cross the exercise yard toward the fence, look around again, then start to climb, my body moving as if I have no control over it, as if it knows what to do. I reach the top of the fence, look across to the outer wall, but there's no one there. I slide over the mesh but under the barbed wire, feeling its razor blades lightly scratching the backs of my thighs. I start to drop down the other side and suddenly feel my feet on the earth once again.

I look left, right, wonder if I'm being watched. I can't hear anything, can't see anything, just the long line of the blank wall stretching out on either side of me, the barbed wire up above it, the stars above that. I walk toward it quickly, my eyes scanning the ground. Eliot said he'd leave a rock there, where the paint was. I scan, scan, but it's so dark, despite the moon. There's nothing to be seen. I walk along the wall a little but there's nothing. I can feel a panic start to rise. I'll have to go back. If the rock's not here, I can't find the paint, and if I can't find it, all this will be for nothing. I walk back farther on the other side. Nothing.

I start to turn in the darkness, and just as I do, the moon comes out a little, and from the corner of my eye I can see a shape next to the wall. A rock. I walk toward it, my shoulders sinking with relief. I crouch down, start to dig under it, push my fingers into the dry earth, but there's nothing. I start to breathe heavily, there's nothing but dust and more dust, and then I think it must've been moved, someone must've kicked it, or moved it, but it couldn't have been kicked far. I look around, examine the soil, there are some undulations nearby but then again, the soil is so dry here, and it blows around, that wouldn't mean anything. I decide to poke about a little before turning back to the bunkhouse and bend over, pushing, pushing, feeling for something, anything, and my fingers find something hard in the soil. I kneel down and start to dig, pull the dust away with my hands, and feel the comforting touch of a brush.

I don't have anywhere to mix the colors; they will have to be mixed wet on the wall. I have four brushes and nowhere to wash them, so I will have to start with the light paint and work toward the dark, which is opposite to the way I'd usually work, and I've already taken too long. I lay the paint tubes out, open them, squirt some onto one of the brushes, and start to get the shapes in place. I outline quickly, my arms and mind taking over. I can hear the brush snag on the rough wall, the sound of the thickness of the paint.

The more I work, the more I disappear. It's like I'm not here anymore, I've gone somewhere else, where my mind is working something out and I don't know how it's doing it and all I can do is let it happen, let it flow like water, and I wonder if everyone who paints feels like that or if Eliot's father felt like that when he played guitar or if Ruth felt like that when she read. And it is only the second time since I came here that I rest. Rest within something that is shielding me from the world, something that's talking for me, telling the world what I need it to, but I do not have to do it, it is doing that for me.

I change brushes, try some darker colors. Images have been coming to me for days, what I could paint. Angry images, all red and crimson, vermilion and cadmium of loss and blood and rocks being thrown, and Deva being dragged away, and spiteful images of Mother Clement in Aureolin Yellow and orange, and then these despairing shadows in Lamp Black and Prussian Blue, but then they dissipated and left me and all I had left was this one image.

I paint and paint, finding my way, building up the color and the shadows, quickly, quickly, and even though I'm tired, my arm is strong from brushing. I smile as I think of this, how pleasing it is.

There's a lot of surface, and the brushes, although

bigger, aren't quite big enough to cover ground fast. I start the detail, working from light to dark, and I'm almost done when I hear a noise and freeze. Vehicles. I turn my head and listen, and I swear I can hear my own heartbeat.

I look down at the mess of tubes and lids at my feet. I hold my breath. It must be Father Renatus coming home, the scrape of metal gates in the distance. I turn back to the wall; the painting must be finished, whatever happens. I quickly assess what needs to be done and finish frantically, get the paint on the wall, and stand back a moment. It will have to do.

I'm sweating, the dust settling in every pore. I crouch by the paint, screw the lids back on, and this time, I can feel my hands shaking, not from the nerves but from tiredness, the adrenaline flagging. My fingers are numb as if I have no control over them, and the more I try, the more I fail. I give up. I'll have to bury everything anyway. I walk along the wall a little, so that they're not buried right by the painting, and start to dig. I run backward and forward, my heart in my mouth, and bury everything, trying to count the lids, count the brushes, trying not to leave anything incriminating behind. I can hear voices in the distance and the hairs on the back of my neck bristle. I pad the sole of my foot over the earth to even it out, try to disguise the fact that it has been disturbed, and then I turn, run as smoothly and as quietly as I can toward the fence.

I look across, the voices getting nearer. They're too close. I listen as two guards chat, and to my horror I realize that it's getting lighter, the darkness thinning a little. It's as if the guards have stopped, are passing a little time. I stand, every nerve on edge, until they start to move away. As the voices get quieter, I begin to climb, find my way over the top of the mesh, but as I drop down the other side, I realize just how much lighter it's getting. I should move slowly, carefully, but there's no time. I run, reach the door, pick up the keys, and try to control my breathing and listen for a moment to make sure it's quiet inside.

I slide the door open and turn my head slowly to see Mother Clement still sleeping. I exhale and slide the door closed again and decide to leave the keys on the floor next to her. They could have dropped off in her sleep. I crouch down, let the keys drop through my fingers slowly, slowly, until they land on the floor with the gentlest of clinks. I get up, look back toward the bunk. I should wash, but it's getting light. I have no idea if I have paint on my arms, on my hands, but I can't risk it. It'll have to wait. It'll have to wait until morning.

28.

It's quiet, peaceful, as I lie with my eyes closed, barely conscious, in the freedom between sleep and awake. My body feels heavy, my mind blank, and I can't think of anything except the sensation of lying here, my chest moving in and out with each breath, in and out, and in and out.

Then a murmuring starts. Nothing loud, just a slight change of energy, a vibration, a sound almost like I imagine bees would make upon exiting a hive. An insistent humming that signals a shift. It gets louder but I keep my eyes closed, block it out, and I'm under those dappled trees where my mother dreamed of sitting and I can hear the bees and it makes me feel warm and tired and I'm squinting my eyes at the sun coming through the canopy of fresh green leaves and there's this gentle breeze that moves the hairs around my face. It's getting louder again and Cass's movement as she drops down from the bunk above me seems to pull me toward consciousness. The sound of bunks creaking and feet on the floorboards and whispering now, and a balance tips and I'm suddenly awake. My mind going back to last night. I open my eyes, stare at Cass's empty bunk, and lie still for a few moments, listening, listening as the humming outside gets louder. I get up, pull on my dress and apron, and run outside.

I don't know what I was expecting but it wasn't this. The yard is filled with girls, all standing in their work dresses and aprons and their bare feet, and they're all facing the wall and there's this frightening silence. I weave through them, searching for Cass's red hair and I find it behind Zuri, all the girls looking through the mesh enclosure toward the perimeter wall, and there it is, in the light of day, and I know, I know why they're quiet. They're looking at the painting on the wall of the Mother sitting at the table, which is overflowing with apples and pears and peaches and plump pink-cheeked babies, her face serene and content as she slices an apple with a knife. I look at Cass, but her eyes are drawn under the table where a young girl with dark smudges under her eyes is kneeling emaciated among rotten fruit. She is knee deep in brown and decayed apples and in her hands is a brush. One hand at either end of it, and she's looking at it in concentration. I don't know what I was expecting, but as I look around, some of the girls are crying, these horrible tears that feel deep and unconscious and stream down their faces. Some of them look at the ground, their feet, their hands, and for the first time in a long time, I'm scared.

I'm scared because the truth is painful and hurts more than all the lies they have been telling us, and suddenly there's screaming, and girls are running at the Mothers, and I see two girls start to drag at Mother Clement's dress and pull her to the floor, and this gasp goes up as Mother Jackson and some of the others start to scream and shout and the guards come running and I don't know what's happening until there's a gunshot above and everyone falls silent, deadly silent, and that's when I see Zuri move. She's turned around to face everyone, her expression difficult to read, but she's reached into her apron, and she has a brush in her hand, and she raises it above her head. My heart's racing and I can feel Cass tense up by my side.

"Enough!" Zuri shouts, her voice coming from deep inside her. It reverberates around us. Her hand is shaking as she's grasping the brush so tightly, and then she holds out the brush in front of her and snaps it, breaks it in two, drops it to the floor. I gasp, and as I look at her, I can hear another snap behind me, and I turn to see a girl from the next bunkhouse do the same. My skin begins to prickle as all around me, girls start to take out their brushes and break them.

"Enough," says another girl.

My mind is reeling.

"Enough!"

"Enough!"

"ENOUGH!"

Their voices come from near and far and it's a strange, musical sound. "Enough!"

And then Cass looks at me, fumbles in her apron, and looks at the brush in her hand, her fingers shaking, her breathing heavy, and she looks at it and grasps it in both hands and snaps it in two and looks up at me and I look for my brush and it's only then that the gunshots come, to frighten us. To shock us. But the breaking, the casting away, does not stop.

"Enough."

"Enough."

More and more guards come running, they open the gate and come into the exercise yard and start to file around us, but then one by one, the girls begin to sit down and the noise changes, they're jeering, shouting. I look around and one after the other they sit. Emily and Zuri and Katie and Rhiannon and I feel a tug on my arm and it's Cass and she's pulling me down and I don't know what's happening until everyone is seated except a few girls, Charmian, the Mothers, the guards, and the noise in indescribable, it's like wailing, shouting, protesting, and grief all in one and you can see on the faces of the guards that they don't know what to do. They fire into the air, but the girls hold hands. The guards shout and kick the girls nearest the edges, but the girls don't move. Cass holds on to my hand tightly, moves closer to me, and I look up at the guards and recognize one of them as Eliot, on the other side of the yard, trying not to look over.

The Mothers begin to scold us and two of them try to haul a girl to her feet, but the nearest girls wrap their arms around her. The Mothers give up eventually, their faces blazing red with humiliation, and to my horror, one of them spits on the girl. There's a collective jeering at this, a galvanizing feeling, the face on the wall of the Mother eating her fruit in everyone's minds. The way she saw the girl under the table as nothing, and I know none of us will be moving from here anytime soon.

♣ ♣ ♣ ♣

It has been a few hours, but the girls are still in high spirits, many of them savoring the energy of rebellion for the first time. Charmian and her friends walked back to the bunkhouses, refused to sit, around ten of their outer circle did too. But everyone else stayed and I'm proud of that. Eliot is still standing guard and the girls are laughing and talking about the novelty of what's happening, not noticing perhaps that the Mothers have disappeared, leaving through the gate toward the main buildings. I know Eliot will have noticed; he knows that they're strategizing. The trucks beyond the fence are ready to go, but there's no one on them. The sun is climbing in the sky, and I can feel the warmth begin to settle in. I look toward Zuri, who's facing me, and she holds my gaze. I nod at her slightly.

"What's going to happen?" It's Cass.

I don't look at her, just feel her presence next to mine. "I don't know," I confess.

I hadn't seen things going this way, but I know they're probably thinking about how to manage the situation. They could try to divide us, or they could start shooting us, but I doubt they'd do that—they need us, and it would be so extreme and so shocking that it would jeopardize getting everyone back to work quickly. I know there's an easier way for them to overcome this rebellion, and they would not have to do a single thing.

"Father Renatus will come, won't he?" mutters Cass. "He'll have to come, and he'll have to listen."

"He'll have to listen," repeats Katie next to Cass.

I bite my tongue. They think they can reason with him.

"Who do you think painted it?" asks Katie, her eyes wide. "Xiao said it was Adaline." Cass doesn't look at me and Zuri looks away.

"They'll kill them, whoever they are."

I try not to move, try not to show anything in my face.

"Can you imagine being them? Here? Now?" says Emily. "But maybe they've given us a chance to make a point. Have more give and take?"

"We'll just have to wait and see what they do," says Zuri.

"And what if they don't do anything?" I ask, the question having been circling in my mind for the past few hours.

"Then we'll have to think again," she says.

I look up as a guard comes near, and we have to keep quiet.

Mum said that there's a way of breaking someone, a formula that they use. Physical discomfort, psychological torture, a mix of both, so that you start to forget what you're fighting for. I already know what they'll do. They give us just enough food to brush, to come into our monthly cycles but no more. We're already weak, and I find myself holding Cass's arm tighter. It's getting hot now, the sun directly overhead, and I know what's coming and make a quick calculation. We're already hungry, thirsty. I look across at Eliot and he's staring straight ahead at us.

After another hour, a truck draws near outside the mesh fence by the painting and a few guards jump off to clean the wall and I watch them, my head getting warm without my hat. I think about the composition, how the book Ruth had showed you how to place items on a table—apples, vases with water or flowers. and they called it "still life." A whole style of painting that was dedicated to observing things, and it said you needed four things of different shapes and then you'd kind of put them together so they'd look good, but the most important thing was to decide where the light was coming from. You had to know where the light was coming from because that was what let you create the shadows, or a thing called "chiaroscuro," so that you could create contrast between the light and the dark, and Ruth's book said that that's what made objects and things seem real. The light gave them weight, and I can't stop thinking about that as they start to splash chemicals on the wall to dissolve the paints, and everyone is watching as they begin to scrub away the forms, the light, the dark, and they work in unison, professionally, until all that is left is a cloud of vague color, a kind of dream where an image had been.

The girls have gone quiet, the heat beginning to bite, and I watch as the guards get back on the truck until one stops, kicks at something, and my heart jumps. I see him bend down, scratch at the earth, and then he picks up a tube of paint, shouts to the others, and they all stand there, kicking about in the earth until the brushes are unearthed, the paints too. They might trace those tubes back to the factory, try to figure out who was on duty in the area; they'll know that someone in the Brush House made the brushes. I sit still, look straight in front of me, my jaw set, and try not to look over at Eliot.

29.

They leave us outside all day. Some of the girls wet themselves and there's a stench of sweat and urine. The girls have quieted down as the guards hoped they would, the energy of the morning flattening. Cass's back slumps as she sits, and just as it begins to get dark, the guards swap over and new guards come on duty, every move calculated to show us that they can sustain this standoff indefinitely.

I watch as Mother Clement and Mother Jackson move toward the exercise yard, wait for a guard to open the gate, and walk without looking at us toward the bunkhouse. Mother Clement rattles her keys and makes sure that we know that she's locking the door. I don't give her the satisfaction of looking over, but after she crosses back, I can see the shapes of Charmian and her friends through the bars of the window. There's a silence as everyone realizes how this is going to go. We'll last fewer than three days without water.

Thankfully it's a clear night, no raging winds, and as we sit, the universe starts to turn above us. The whole sky illuminated by the now-full moon, and I realize that Cass has gone to sleep—she's already weak from not having eaten yesterday, already dehydrated, and I find my decision to let her sleep yesterday gnawing at me. Some other girls are leaning their heads on their friend's shoulders too, and it's deadly quiet, the initial euphoria dissolving as the physical discomfort starts to make its presence felt.

"We should've organized," Zuri says. "We should've stayed inside, or if we were going to try to overwhelm them, we should've spread the word, done it right. . . ."

I look up at her.

"We're too vulnerable here," she says.

I look up and around. We're sitting targets, out in the open.

"Don't say that," says Katie sharply.

"We won't last two days," says Zuri matter-of-factly. "They'll just leave us here until we die or give in."

"I don't know which would be worse," says Emily tetchily.

"We'll have to give up, give in this time," replies Zuri, "let them think they've won. Then we can organize. Get ready for next time. We're only punishing ourselves out here, we're just getting weaker."

"But what if we don't get a chance again?" asks Emily urgently. "They'll be watching us every second from now on."

"Then we'll *make* a chance." Zuri's voice is rising despite herself.

"Zuri's right," I say. "It's a fight we can't win."

"So you're giving up?" snaps Katie.

"It's not that," I say. "We have the power, we're just not going to win this time."

Katie looks at me as if I've lost my mind. Emily laughs bitterly. "Power?"

"Yes," I say. "Without us, there's no brushing; without that, there's no trading. They need our bodies, they need our babies. They're terrified of losing control of us," I say, and I can see Katie thinking, thinking.

I see Zuri's eyes shine in the darkness, Emily's face tense up.

"The problem is that they can withhold water, food, and they'll use it against us. What we have to do is hold on here for as long as we comfortably can," I say. "Make them think we *have* held out, that they're stronger than us, cleverer than us, that they've won. Then we save our strength and make a plan. We know everyone's on board now, well, except Charmian's gang, but there's an appetite for this. All we need to do is channel it the right way. Do we agree?"

I look around, and Zuri nods, then Emily, then eventually Katie, and it's strange, but for the first time I feel part of something, part of these girls, their minds and mine, their hands and mine.

We decide to take it in turns to sleep, Zuri and Katie first, and as the sky clears above us, I watch as Emily begins to look up at the stars.

"Cassiopeia," I say quietly. Emily looks at me, puzzled.

"That shape there." I point it out to her. "There are stories with each shape. Cassiopeia was a girl, her parents sacrificed her."

She looks up, tries to decipher the sky above.

"Sacrificed her to save their country, betrayed her and chained her to a rock under the sea, because she was so alive, because she was so aware of her own beauty."

"And they couldn't have a daughter like that?" she asks sadly.

"No," I say, smiling, "I suppose not." It's then that I look over and realize that her dark eyes are shining with tears.

I have never seen dawn break before, not without bars in the way. The way the darkness thins like dipping water into dark paint, seeing the way the colors diffuse. In the city, the sky was always full of smoke. It's like the light never goes away, but is always present in the darkness, and this morning, it seems to be overcoming the black with shades of pale blue and pink. I watch in wonder and look at Zuri, who has woken by now and is rubbing the sides of her arms, trying to get her blood flowing. The other girls wake one by one and are sullen, desperately hungry and thirsty. I look at Cass, who is slow to stir—I shake her, rub her face, and she eventually comes to, but she's weak. I check her pulse like Ruth taught me once and the beat under my fingertips is erratic. I frown and look over to see Zuri catching my eye.

"I think it's time to call it quits," I say.

"No." It's Cass now. I look at her, she's pale, her eyes inexpressive.

"Cass, you're not well, you won't be able to—"

"Not yet," she interjects, forcing her voice to sound stronger now. "I'm okay. Promise me?"

I look at Zuri, she shrugs, and I look back at Cass. "We'll give it a few more hours....," I compromise, "but no more than that."

Emily starts to whisper into Katie's ear and then Katie passes on the message that we have to stay here for a little longer. There's silence, no belligerence today, no shouting, just a deep, heavy exhaustion.

The Food Hall is open, and we can hear some of the Mothers clattering in the kitchen. They've opened the windows and the doors too to make sure we can smell the food. My eyes turn to Emily, and I can see that she's lightheaded with hunger, and it's strange, but I'm not surprised that this is how they're planning to break us.

Mum said that it was always that way, that they would say they'd change and then offer you the same, make you think that it is the best choice, make you grateful for it. It would seem to suit the character of Father Renatus too. The way he effortlessly conveys that everything is done for us, the chiding tone of his words, the barely concealed contempt for us and everything that we are. No one moves, and I stare at the wall on the other side of the mesh. Eventually the Food Hall doors close again, and Charmian and her friends walk back to the bunkhouse. I can't look over at them, and wait until they disappear.

It's even hotter today, and there's a wind that has begun to disturb the earth around us, and some of the girls are coughing, one so much so that she begins to retch. I catch the eye of a girl called Isla, and despite her exhaustion, she gives me a soft smile. She broke her brush and so did the girl behind her, and it seems like there's been this feeling that has bubbled up and overflown. An idea or a thought passed around so that they're seeing things differently. There's a commotion now as the girl who was coughing passes out and the girls look up at the guards to see them standing motionless, having obviously been given their orders.

Throughout the day the situation is repeated over and

over. The despair spreads like poison between the girls, and under the scorching midday sun, one of the girls begins to cry. I look behind me to find the little girl that I keep seeing and she's bowing her head, her eyes far away and she's being so brave but my heart bleeds for her. Cass is asleep again and the heat is making my thoughts melt. It's like everything is far away, as if I've separated my body and my mind, and my head aches in a way I've never felt before. I try to straighten out my legs, but they're cramped, shooting pains making their way toward my thighs, and more girls begin to sob. I set my jaw and try to exist in that moment, the way we are, and it's then, just as the heat of the day begins to lessen, a truck arrives outside the gate and the bunkhouse door is opened.

Charmian is led across the exercise yard with a guard, her eyes on the truck, and the gate closes behind her. I look at Zuri, who is trying to keep her eyes open. Charmian turns her nose at the stench of us human animals—our sweat, our urine—and I look around at the broken brushes strewn over the ground and I think of the only time I saw Mum despair. It wasn't because she was left alone to raise us, or that she had to give us this world to live in, it wasn't even not having food or coming home to find that intruders had taken things from the house. It was when I collected up all those paintings I did of her and showed her them all together, all the lives she could have lived, and I saw something in her eyes that scared me. That she could imagine them and that although that was sometimes a great comfort, it could cause so much pain too. It was only fleeting, but I felt it pass through the room like a cold draft before leaving again.

I close my eyes and hold Cass's hand and try not to think about how thirsty I am. How dry my mouth and throat are, even the surface of my eyes. I wait, listen, squeeze Cass's hand every now and again to make sure that she's still warm, and then there's the sound of the truck again, and the screeching of the gate, and through the darkening night comes Charmian. Her shoulders broad, her gait steady. She walks toward us.

"Father Renatus wants me to tell you that he appreciates that you work hard. He says that you are right, you deserve more rest. One day a week and more food, a third more. He wants you to know that he cares about you."

"So where is he?" comes a voice.

"He's busy trying to find ways to get more food for you. Working all the time. All that he asks is that you meet him halfway. Work as hard as he does."

I can feel the resolve of some of the girls soften.

"He wants you to know that there's water in the Food Hall for you. Clean clothes on your bunks. He said that there'll be food in the morning and that he's happy to forget all of this."

As she finishes speaking, the doors of the Food Hall open, and I look at Zuri, and she knows, and I know that it's over.

"It's okay," she mouths. "This is just for now." I look at her, nod slightly.

"We just need to gather our strength," she says again, and I nod back at her, tears in my eyes.

30.

Cass brought up the first cup of water and the second, all over the front of her dress. I stood beside her, trying to hold her up, but all I could see were stars. There was nothing to eat, so we walked back to the bunkhouses to wash. We cross the bunkhouse now and listen to the murmur of the girls, somewhat revived by the bitter water. There's a palpable physical relief among some of them, a fragile triumph in some of the girls' eyes. A sense that they had achieved something, and then I hear Charmian's voice behind me cool and calm, pleased with herself.

"Look at you," she says. "Look at the state of you."

I don't react, just keep walking as Cass heads straight for her bunk. I don't have the strength to counter Charmian, and she knows it, and I feel a tug at my shoulder. I swing around, try to bring her into focus.

"Say thank you, then. . . ."

Her eyes are bright, her face elated, she raises an eyebrow. Her friends come and gather around her to enjoy this moment.

"Come on. . . ." She smiles. "Say thank you, Charmian."

I look away and she reaches out and grabs my chin and I cannot pull away. She digs her nails into the sides of my face.

"Say thank you for everything I did for you." Her smile is menacing now. I push her arm away and she laughs, her friends do too.

"I want you to remember this," she says, "the favor I did you tonight. I want you to remember that I sorted this out. If it wasn't for me, you'd all be dead by now."

I try to find words but I don't have any, and then she pushes me and it is everything I can do to not fall over and there's this laughter and then I feel Emily behind me, holding me up, and she walks with me back to my bunk, pulls the dress over my head.

"You need to sleep," she says, and then her eyes dart to a smear of paint on the inside of my forearm, and she stops, looks around, and starts to scrape it off with her nail. I watch her and am thankful that it's dark and then I lie down and there's nothing left inside of me and all I can see is Cass's hair over the side of the bunk, hanging down as it always has, and then it goes black.

There is more food than usual in the morning, I knew there would be, at least for a few days, just long enough to keep us feeling like we achieved something. Cass eats hungrily and I soak the bread in the water so that it is easier to swallow. The girls are quiet this morning, exhausted, their resolve tested. After we're done eating, we walk back to the bunkhouse to fetch our hats, and across the yard there's a different kind of noise, the sound of guards, trucks, hammering. They're building a higher fence around the mesh. My stomach sinks and Cass touches my shoulder. We get our hats, and as we walk out, we see Charmian still lying on her bunk. Mother Jackson sees her there, and despite the fact that we all need to be getting to work, she doesn't say anything to her.

Charmian looks up and smiles at us. "Enjoy your work," she says.

Cass looks over, searches my face, and we silently conclude that this must be her reward, along with the extra food that lies on the sheet of her bunk.

Cass and I wait by a truck and watch as the guard hands out spare brushes to the girls, and then Zuri comes to get me.

"They need us in the Brush House to replace all those broken brushes," she says, her voice revealing nothing. I nod, look at Cass, and she smiles softly at Zuri and me.

"I'll be fine," she says, but I'm not sure she's even convincing herself.

I follow Zuri back to the bunkhouse and find the seven or eight other girls who work in the Brush House alongside Katie and Xiao. We wait for Mother Clement, and when she comes, we follow her as usual across the exercise yard, but instead of going to the Brush House, she veers off to the right, past the Mothers' House and toward the main buildings. I can feel Zuri's tension in her body in front of me as we walk in a line toward the Assembly Hall. Mother Clement pushes open the door, and our footsteps seem noisy in the cavernous room without the hundreds of other girls, and then my eyes adjust to the dimness, and to my panic I see

Father Renatus standing there, a girl by his side, her back to us. I look at her, confused, a strange familiarity about her. My mind tries to work it out and it's then that she turns. It's Emily. She stands, her eyes unable to meet mine, jutting out her chin defiantly. The skin on her neck is blotchy and my mind starts to race. Her "curiosity" about Cass and Deva, the way she was posted to the Brush House after the first painting, the way she held my arm as she scraped off the paint with her fingernail last night, the way she looked at me through the dark.

"Line up, quickly," barks Mother Clement, her eyes going toward Father Renatus as he walks toward us, and I can feel the other girls shrink. He smiles, and since he isn't on the stage, I realize how short he is in reality. He stares at us, takes us in, and walks the line for a moment, his shoes squeaking on the floor. He pauses.

"I've been speaking to my friend Emily," he says softly. She drops her eyes now, painfully conscious of all our eyes on her, and I feel this horrible, out-of-control anger, hot and spitting. I know Zuri feels it too, and Katie. We're done for. She knows what we did. I look across at the guards by the door and suddenly my mind is filled with Willow's friend's screams, and my legs want to run, I want to get out. This is it.

"She very kindly keeps an eye on things. For example, she brought a rather inappropriate relationship between two girls to my attention."

I think it's hate, what I'm feeling, something dark and scary.

"And more recently, some paints were found," he says

softly. There's a sheen of grease on his skin, it glistens on his cheekbones, under the puffiness of his gray eyes. He keeps walking back and forth as if to convey the agitation that's not audible in his voice.

"And some brushes, unusual ones . . . they were so big." He stops walking now, laughs, and scratches his head.

"The thing is, as you know, you are the ones that make the brushes, and I wanted to know if you knew anything about them?"

I look straight ahead, breathe, try not to draw attention to myself with any stiffening of my body or clenching of my teeth. This is a trap; it is a trap.

"Of course, we have no evidence that the brushes were made and hidden by one of you, but it seems the most likely explanation, and it's perfectly obvious that this person needs our help, so if any of you can give me a name, I'd be very grateful." He knows, he already knows, and he's just waiting to see if we will confess. He needs that victory. He scans our faces now, waits, and in the background, I can still hear the fence being built higher around the exercise yard.

"Xiao?" he asks, his head turned to the side. "Do you want to tell me anything?"

Xiao, who always looks so confident, so at ease, starts to stutter. "I-I don't know, sir. No, sir. I promise."

He stares at her for a long time, making her suffer.

"Very well," he says eventually, and steps down the line.

Emily is crying now, sniffing, and I'm glad that she is, I'm glad that she's hurting for all that she's done.

"How about you, Katie?"

Katie looks terrified, singled out. "I'm sorry, I . . . there's nothing. I don't know anything, sir."

Emily has told him, and he wants me to say it. That is what will give him the satisfaction, because it's all about breaking us, like Mum said, and suddenly I can feel her with me. Her eyes, her hands, her heart beating in mine, and I feel something else rising within me, something that belongs to her, defiance perhaps, but more than that—a refusal to let him make me do something I don't want to do—and then, he's in front of me.

"Ah, you, our latecomer. . . ." He fixes me with his slate eyes, and then, to my horror, he moves toward me, reaches out his pasty hand, and tugs the end of my shorter hair.

"Your mother was quite the rebel, wasn't she?" He hasn't let my hair go. I feel sick with the thought of him saying anything about my mother.

He cocks his head. "I wonder if rebellion runs in the genes?" he asks, and his hand is near my face now. "Tell me," he says, his warm breath on my face, "Do you want to confess anything?"

I can see the color of his eyes and they are lifeless, dead, like the ones I used to draw when I first started drawing eyes. No spark, no color. I look at him, think of my mother.

"NO," I say, my voice steady. He looks at me, lets go of my hair, and puts his finger under my chin, examines the angles of my face.

"So you know nothing about this?"

"No, sir," I say, and resist the urge to spit in his face. He waits a moment, and I want to scream, to push him away, every cell in my body revolted by him.

"Very well," he says again, and continues down the line, and I look up, across at Emily, who's still looking at the floor.

At the end of the line, he turns and walks back. He looks a little irritated now, the lack of control riling him, and suddenly I consider Emily again. He glances across at her.

"I have told Emily, and I will tell you, that I would be willing for the first girl to tell me who was responsible for those brushes to be relieved of her duties, and as a gesture of my personal thanks, she would be allowed to leave the camp, be allowed to have light duties in the offices of the military, and choose her life partner."

The words fall heavily around us. No one has ever been allowed to leave and there is no bigger prize than to be given your freedom. I've heard rumors that some of the general's daughters are offered this. I stand, my stomach sinking, and I suddenly realize that Emily has not said anything about me. This was a ruse, to get us to talk. It seems she is an informant, but she has not said anything. I feel this warmth flow over my body—relief, adrenaline—and then his face hardens.

"My door is always open," he says, "and the first girl, and *only* the first girl, will be allowed to leave." He waits for a moment, looks at our faces, and then there's an almost interminable pause.

"Well," he says eventually, "you'd better get back to work."

The girls are eager to escape, but as we turn to leave, his voice cuts across our footsteps. We look back.

"The thing is, we know some of you are lying, and when we find out who, I cannot stress how awful the consequences will be."

31.

There are two more guards in the Brush House to make four when we arrive back, but Eliot isn't one of them. The younger of the two of them has his head shaved, a scar above his eye, the other is older with cold eyes. Zuri and I get to work, and I notice that Zuri's hands are shaking. I lean across, hold her hand for a moment and I watch as she takes a deep inhale and exhale. I want to talk to her, I need to talk to her about Emily, about the way she came into our confidence, the ease with which she did it and how gullible we, *I*, had been, and I'm angry and I can't think and I thought I knew better.

"Oi!" comes the voice of one of the younger guards as he moves toward us and you can tell by his restlessness that they have been given strict orders to watch us. I let go of Zuri's hand, go back to trying to wind the string on the brush, but my hand is shaking, and then we hear the door open, and Emily comes in. I don't look at her as she takes her place, and I feel the strange self-consciousness of ignoring someone's presence. The way you become aware of your every movement and theirs, how you somehow pay more attention to them as you're trying to pretend they don't exist.

Mum had warned me about trusting people too readily, she knew how dangerous it could be. She told me enough times, but when there's a friendly face in front of you, when you think you see a truth in someone, how can you not trust them? It's almost chemical or something, perhaps like falling in love. I try to steady my hand, wind the string, try to concentrate on wrapping it neatly so I have a focus, but my mind keeps bleeding like paint to what could have happened this morning and suddenly I feel this coldness through me. Images of Zuri being dragged away, the guard's hands tight around my wrists, my heels dragging, the screaming, and I find myself closing my eyes to block it all out.

"Get on with it!" It's the guard again and my eyes snap open. They will be watching us now, every moment of every day. Here, in the bunks, in the Assembly Hall, there will be eyes everywhere, and the higher fence around the exercise yard will soon be finished.

A revolution is too dangerous. I thought I knew how dangerous it was, but it wasn't until I felt that terror walking its way slowly up my spine in the Assembly Hall that I realized what it really meant. To be hurt myself was one thing, to see Zuri, Katie hurt . . . Cass?

I force myself to breathe, wind another brush, keep my eyes on the work.

Mum said that they used the same tactics when people were protesting. Someone new would join and you'd get a good feeling about them and everything would go well and then suddenly, out of nowhere, someone you knew would get arrested, jailed, until you couldn't trust anyone, until you couldn't talk to anyone, and the point was not to make you think your friend was an informant, it was to make you think that *anyone* could be.

♣ ♣ ♣

The day drags on under a cloak of anxiety and suspicion, counting the seconds until I can get out to the exercise yard. My mind going over the seconds and minutes and hours in the way it does when it's trying to soothe itself.

"Are you okay?" It's Eliot.

I sit, my back against the mesh, the taller fence another layer between us.

"I don't know," I answer honestly. There's a deep silence.

"I don't really know what I thought might happen, but it wasn't that," I say. "I just wanted to move them. But I feel like we wasted an opportunity, probably the last one we'll have." Then I fall silent. There are just so many things, so many words, but I don't know where to start.

"Jess?" he says after a while. "You're frightening me."

"They found the brushes. Father Renatus called us to the Assembly Hall."

"What?" He sounds shocked now.

"It's okay, he didn't know anything, but for a moment there, I thought they had us, I thought . . ."

He's quiet now, thinking.

"I thought the girls would see," I say, "but then they were so happy just to have a little more water, a little more rest. I thought they'd want more."

"You're . . . *we're* asking a lot from them . . . to go against everything they know, everything they've been made to believe."

My mind goes to Emily, the way she tried to catch up with Zuri and me on the way back from the Brush House. "The thing I don't understand is that some of them are holding the whole system up. . . ."

"Only because it gives them power they don't feel. It's an illusion. Those girls informing? It makes them feel safer. It makes them believe that they're on the inside. They do it because they're scared."

"Maybe," I say, my eyes going to the ground, the soil, the dust.

"I'll never get over the fence to paint again," I say quietly. I can hear him think about this.

"Maybe you don't need to. . . . ," he says. "You already lit a match, the fire has already taken hold. Now we just need to blow on the flames."

Despite myself, my skin prickles at this.

"They're letting me drive now," he says, his voice getting more animated. "So many soldiers have been injured in the riots, they've needed more drivers."

I listen to his voice, know he's going somewhere with this.

"And as long as I'm in a camp vehicle, with my uniform, I can get through gates, get across checkpoints."

Despite my tiredness, my mind starts to whir.

"I could get you out of the camp," he says. "We could get across the city limit checkpoint. Cass, Zuri, as many as we can. We'd be free."

The way he says it is so simple.

"I've got all the paperwork ready. I've found some old license plates to swap, they'd never trace us. We could find your mother."

I feel the tears prick at the corners of my eyes.

"I wanted you to know you've given me hope, Jess," he says quietly. "When things get bad, I think of that painting and I . . ." He stops. "I don't know, I feel different, I feel that there's a different life to fight for . . . hope."

I listen.

"And I wanted you to know too that I heard Deva is still in the city."

"What?" I fight the desperate urge to turn around, to get up, her name a small light in the darkness.

"Don't get too excited, but I heard she was taken to be a military cook at the main depot in the city, they might move her, but she was well, last time she was seen. I'll do my best to find out more."

I try to take this in. See in my mind a flicker of Cass's delighted face when I tell her.

And then a wave of tiredness washes through me, a tension I hadn't known was being held so tightly inside. I get up, brush down my skirt. "I need to tell Cass," I say.

"Sure," he says, and I start to walk away. "Jess?"

I stop.

"Don't give up, okay?"

I stand, my back to him. "I won't," I say.

"No, I mean it," he says. "I don't have many friends, and I can't lose you. You have to promise."

I pause.

"I promise," I hear myself say, although my heart is still unsure.

32.

There are definitely fewer blossoms and when I touch the flowers with my brush, they seem to fall apart. I'm with Zuri today and she's restless, catching my eye every minute through the tree. "In my grandmother's favorite book, she said there was a woman called Janie." I look across at her now.

"She burns her head rags because this man is jealous of her, of everything she is, everything she can be."

I listen to her as she talks, a certain preoccupation about her. "I don't understand," I say.

"There's a stove in the Brush House for the hot glue," she says, her voice urgent. "I can't believe I hadn't noticed it before."

I know the one she's talking about, it heats up the chemical glue we use for the brushes and stops it from drying.

"There's a lighter there, on the shelf, they use it to light the gas." Her eyes are dancing now.

"We only need one, we can pass it around, set the mattresses and our work dresses alight." I can feel the energy radiating from her.

"It would be too dangerous to leave us inside. They'll have to let us out, that could be our chance. . . ."

My mind goes to Eliot, and his truck. She's studying my face now.

"What happened with Emily, it wasn't our fault, we couldn't know," she reminds me. I keep brushing, try not to look at her.

"Jess?" she asks. "Say something."

I look back at her now, can feel the tears catching in my throat. "Zuri, you were in the Assembly Hall with me, we were this close to being caught," I say.

She lowers her brush, and I look away. There's an uncomfortable silence between us.

"Jess, look at me," she says finally. And when I do I realize she's begun shaking, her eyes intense.

"Don't you dare go putting dreams in our heads and then get scared. You did this," she says, emphasizing every single word, "and you're going to finish it, along with us. Now is not the time to start doubting yourself."

I feel this anger starting to rise. "But I don't know who we can trust, Zuri! I don't know how far the others will go. There are more guards now, everyone's watching."

"You can't dangle this dream and then take it away, Jess. Stop thinking, it's time for doing. We need to get out of here before we all die of heat exhaustion, of boredom, of childbirth, and who knows what else. . . ."

I have never seen her so alive.

"We are going to do this, and we are going to get out of here. If we die trying, then so be it, because I know that this is not enough for you, and it certainly is not enough for me. I deserve more, so much more."

I feel my cheeks burn with shame.

"You can't let us down, Jess. You cannot let me down."

We're looking at each other now, through these threadbare blossoms. I consider her face.

"I'm sorry," I say quietly.

She exhales, and I can see her frame soften a little. "It's okay," she says. "It's okay to get scared, but we don't let fear win."

We stretch our hands across to each other for just a moment.

"We just need to choose the right time, set the bunks on fire, and we'll need to prepare, properly. We'll need wedding gowns."

I look at her in confusion.

"For the journey out. If we're going out, we'll need to wear them. You, me, Cass . . ." She almost says "Emily" out of force of habit.

"We'll need to hide them after laundry day," she says, "under the mattresses." I nod. Smile. She's worked everything out.

"Jess, together we can do this. When we've got everything in place. We'll just have to choose our moment." She looks at me seriously, the tip of her brush coming away from the tree as she thinks.

"We'll know when it's time," she says, and as I look at the certainty in her face, I believe her.

The guard is walking the line of trees now and we get back to work, my mind going back to the Brush House, the lighter. It's strange, but I've always been afraid of fire, of its heat, it always seemed to be part of something destructive. The riots in the city, the burning out of houses, the wildfires that seemed to rage across the world, burning everything in their paths. I remember Shey saying that it must have once been a great gift, and I couldn't understand, and then I thought about those early people and how much they valued fire. The simple warmth, the light, and I wonder if we'll ever think of it like that again. I suppose so many meanings have changed. A storm is not what it was, fire is different, water does not clean you, love doesn't matter anymore, and life itself is not lived. Perhaps we'll need a new language, perhaps we'll destroy that too and make words meaningless so that all we can do is exist in silence.

I watch Zuri now, her face determined, purposeful, and slowly I can feel the heaviness start to lift inside me.

I eat with Cass tonight. Since hearing that Deva is in the city, there's a shade of lightness in her face, she's eating more too, and her face looks a little less strained. She has said that she will volunteer for laundry as she isn't in the Brush House so isn't being watched as much. She's quiet, though, the relief of knowing Deva is well still tempered with her anxiousness about when she'll see her again. I leave her at the table as Zuri joins her. I walk out to the exercise yard.

"Jess?" It's Emily. I can feel my body tense and my steps get quicker.

"Jess, please, you've got to talk to me sometime."

I feel her hand on my arm. "Let me go!" I shake her off.

"Jess, please . . ."

I carry on walking though I'm not sure to where; there's no way to really get away from her.

"They said they'd give my brother more time at home, with my mother."

The words reach me through the darkness and I stop. I stand, my back to her. She's sobbing. "They said they'd let him have another year if I kept an eye out. He's only ten, Jess."

My head drops, and I turn to face her.

"He's just a kid," she says again, pressing the tears from her face roughly with the palms of her hands. "I'm sorry."

"You told them about Cass and Deva," I say, my voice charged. She doesn't say anything, there's nothing she *can* say.

"They already knew, there was no point in me lying," she says. "Once Cass reacted like that when Deva took ill, they knew."

I start to turn and walk away.

"Jess, please . . . I didn't tell them anything about the paint."

"Just shut up!" I turn in anger. "What the hell is wrong with you?"

She is desperate, I can see it in her eyes, her voice getting louder and louder. "I didn't say anything about any plan or anything."

"Will you be quiet!" I press my hand on her mouth and she's breathing hard and I suddenly know why I can't look her in the eye and then I can't stop myself. "You are everything I don't understand," I say, pushing out the words between my teeth. "You are the type that just goes along with things, the type who does one thing and says another, anything to make your life easier, anything to make your life better." I can feel this anger bubbling up through me as everyone like Emily seems to flash through my mind, the politicians years ago, the ones who had all the power, the guards as they watched Mum scrabble for food, Mother Clement and her dead eyes, and suddenly I realize that this isn't about Emily. I pull my hand away from her face, and then I can't seem to get any oxygen out of the air and my mind feels fuzzy and there's just a little crying girl in front of me.

"I didn't say anything," she repeats, sadly this time.

"How do I know you didn't say anything?" I ask, my voice more composed.

"Because I wouldn't be here, would I? He said he'd let me go."

"He was only saying that."

"We'll never know. But I couldn't do it, Jess."

I feel suddenly so tired, so unbelievably tired.

She stops crying now, takes a breath. "It was that story you told me about the stars and the painting. . . . I don't know, but it was like I suddenly saw everything in a different way."

I look at her. Her fragile frame. She looks sorry.

"I don't know if I can trust you," I say. "You lied so easily."

"It wasn't easy. I did it for my brother," she says, walking nearer to me. "Don't tell me you wouldn't do the same."

I don't know how to answer that.

"You can trust me," she says. "I can prove it." She moves closer to me still, and as she does, she turns over her arm and pulls up the sleeve of her dress. There in the dark is a metallic triangle—the tip of something. She reaches out and grabs my hand, places it on her arm, and under the thick material, I can feel the long blade of a knife.

"I stole it from the Brush House. I thought it might come in useful." Her eyes are wide now, her breathing fast.

"You can trust me, Jess. I promise."

33.

I slid the knife between the rungs under Cass's bed and every night I look up at it and sometimes, when I know Mother Clement is asleep, I reach up and press my thumb to the blade, thinking about Emily, about the thinness of the steel at the edge and how easy it would be to fall either side of it, and then I think about Shey and the gun they would have given him and what he may or may not do with it.

I had thought that perhaps the knife would start to feel more familiar in my hand, but last night as I held it, it was still cold, dead—so unlike a brush, which seems to become part of me, an extension of me—and I frowned as I looked at it through the darkness, knowing deep down that if it came to it, I would have difficulty using it.

This morning Zuri, Emily, and I are making brushes again, the younger guard walking around us in incessant circles, and even though the shed stinks of chemicals, you can still smell his sweat. We work for an hour or two until the door opens and I catch a glimpse of another guard's uniform and I realize with relief that it is Eliot. I look up and see the first guard stop walking, his whole body bristling as Eliot walks in, an indescribable tension.

Eliot walks to his chair, sits down, and the other guard continues with his walking, giving as much of his attention to Eliot as to us, watching him, trying to intimidate him, and I realize that this is who he has been partnered with, the one he hates so much. I put my head down, try not to check that the lighter is still by the stove.

I could put it in my apron when I move over to wash my hands, but when they put the flame out at the end of the day, they might notice it wasn't there. The other way to do it would be to topple over the whole stove, make a mess, and grab it then, but I could be punished for that. I finish another brush and walk to the sink and rub the alcohol gel on my hands, noticing as I do that my skin is red and raw. I glance over. It is there, just out of reach, a blue plastic oblong with fluid inside. I take my time until the young guard shouts at me, and I smile, turn back toward the table.

We can't talk here anymore, not since the new guards arrived, and the day seems three times as long. I listen as Emily strips more wood with a knife and the peelings curl and fall to the floor.

I asked Mum once whether she had used the knife she kept in the waistband of her jeans, and she said that she had. I could tell that she didn't want to talk about it, so I left it, but then every few years I would remember, and I'd want to know, and I'd ask again. As I grew up, it was like I wanted to know all of her, everything, who she was as a person, all the gnarly twisted bits too, and one night when Shey was asleep, she came to lie on the mattress, and we listened as these gangs shouted in the streets outside. She'd already barricaded the door and she always slept in her clothes just in case, but this time her knife was by her side and she told me about a time when these thugs came into the house, and she had managed to lock us in my room, and they were taking everything, all the food we had, and she said that all she could hear was us crying on the other side of the door, and then when they'd gotten everything they wanted, they sort of stopped and looked at her, and then she knew she was in trouble because it wasn't about things anymore.

I remember us lying there, our faces almost touching, and the darkness above us tinged orange from the fires in the city, and she whispered to me that I was growing up and that when that happened, you began to realize that things could be replaced, but there were things that they could take from you that could not be, and those she would defend with a knife. She said that she slashed one of them across his stomach with her knife as he got closer to her. When she said that, it was almost funny. Not funny in a laughing way, but it was so out of character, so far away from who she was, that I just couldn't understand it. The knife ripped his clothes, nicked his skin, and then she slashed his arm, a deep cut. She said she needed them to know that she was serious, that she would fight, and they started saying that she was mad, and their expressions changed, and they started looking at her in disgust. They called *her* mad when they came into *her* house, took everything *she* had, and tried to hurt her, and then to save their own face, they said that she'd be too much trouble, and they left. Too much trouble, that's what they said as she fought for everything she had.

And it was stupid, but she said she barricaded the door again and she was desperate to let us out of the room, but there was blood on the floor, and she needed to clean that up and it was in that moment I realized that every fight she fought was for us. That there were things that she had to do to keep our minds safe, and I remember holding on to her and feeling her arms around me, and even though there were riots outside still, I knew that she would do anything for me and that I was loved. I pick up another brush and look at it a moment. Perhaps anyone could use a knife if they had to. I look up and catch Emily's eye, and despite myself, I feel my anger softening.

The young guard changes direction again and eyeballs Eliot every time he passes him.

Zuri takes a break to wash her hands, and the young guard follows her over. I catch her eye, and she frowns, continues to rub her hands together. I know what she's thinking. It's too dangerous to try to take the lighter today. I listen as she rubs her hands dry and walks back toward me. I look up at Eliot and he's looking straight ahead. This will be more difficult than we thought.

"I've got them!" It's Cass, her face aglow. When she gets like this, her face lights up, drawing attention to her.

"Okay, calm down," I say warmly. Zuri smiles by my side.

Cass tries to flatten her expression but she's bursting.

She leans over the table. "It wasn't that difficult; I was on the laundry today. I folded them under the sheets on my arm and then put them into the pillowcases."

She's happier than I've seen her in a long time. "It felt incredible," she says, staring at me, and she looks so well. There's a spark of something.

It's then that she looks up and Emily comes to sit with us, carrying a tray. Cass looks over at me, startled, and I can feel Zuri look at me sideways, but I just give them the briefest of shrugs. Cass's smile widens, her love of harmony satisfied.

"This is lovely," she says as she eats her bread hungrily.

We eat in contentment until we're ready to go out to the exercise yard and then we all go and sit together by the fence and there's this quiet and the stars are piercing tonight. Emily looks up at them and Cass is swirling her finger in the soil.

"Do you think we'll make it?" asks Cass quietly. Zuri looks over.

"Of course," she says uncertainly. Everyone's quiet a little longer.

"Jess's mum says there's somewhere else," Cass continues, still trying to get her name right in the soil. "Somewhere in the North where people are starting over."

Emily looks over eagerly. I shrug, embarrassed, but I watch as Zuri pictures it.

I exhale. "My mum used to protest with people, against all this, tried to make them see it wasn't right. They had a plan to find a patch of land, to start again . . . gently."

"I can see it," Zuri says. "And there's a sea you can swim in, and gardens, and you can grow flowers. Beautiful flowers, not just things to eat. . . . ," she whispers.

"And at night"—it's Emily now—"you can sit outside and listen to owls. My mum told me about owls. . . ."

I smile.

"And eat so much food that you could almost burst," adds Cass. "Fruit and coffee and bread . . ."

"No more bread," moans Zuri. "I want stew and jollof rice. I never tried it, but my granddad said it was sooooo good."

And then this contented silence falls on us again as each of us starts to build up these worlds in our minds on this patch of dry earth.

34.

I'm tired today. Cass sits on the floor as I plait her hair, and I can hardly concentrate. She's quiet too. Perhaps we've been spending too much time in this imagined future. I snake lengths of her hair through my fingers, over and under, over and under, so that the plaits stand proud on her head. Her hair is thick, prone to waving, and because of that, it knots at the nape of her neck, so I have to pull it so that she usually yelps, but she's too tired to protest today. I tap her on her shoulders when I'm done, and she's slow to get up. I push her shoulders forward, get up gently, walk around her, and bend down to grab her hands and haul her to her feet.

We get into the wash line, our rags on our shoulders, and I wait for Cass to finish washing. She takes a long time today, but I'm in no rush. Eventually I take my own turn, and we head back to the bunks to pull on our dresses, and as we do so, we pass Charmian laughing on her bunk. She hasn't worked for weeks, and even though I try not to, I find myself glancing at her. She looks different, rested. She sits up as I pass by.

"What are you looking at?"

I try to follow Cass, just ignore her as usual.

"Come on. . . . ," she says. "What is it?"

I turn, look at her, know this won't be easy. Question why I'm even going to do it. "I blamed you for telling them about Cass and Deva. I shouldn't have."

She looks lost, like she doesn't know how to respond. The girls around her are quiet.

She gets up and looks at me squarely and I'm sure she's about to launch her attack, but she just stands there.

"I didn't tell them anything," she says defensively, and I know instinctively that she's telling the truth.

"I know that now, and I just wanted to say I'm sorry."

She gasps, and to my horror, she looks upset. I don't know what to do now either.

"Anyway," I say, and turn to walk away, and I see her from the side of my vision wiping away some tears roughly.

"Whatever," I hear her spit as she walks to the washroom.

We get on the trucks and brush today, the last zone of the season, though that doesn't mean much. I'm sure they make the zones up so that we feel that we've accomplished something. Ruth said that they used to do that where she worked as a nurse—gave you little targets so you felt good about reaching them. In reality they didn't mean much, but they kept everyone together and working hard. I listen to the metal gates scrape along the ground and the guards yelling. Cass leans her head on my shoulder and I look out toward the North as we drive.

It's a good day today for brushing and we're on almonds and Cass is opposite me and there's this blueness to the sky that there hasn't been for a while and I think of the painting I saw of almond blossoms by a man called Monet or Van Gogh or something and I remember Ruth saying that the man loved the blossoms because they were so clean and fresh and full of this sense of waking up and the start of new life and I look across at Cass and there are these wisps of hair around her face and she looks like she exists outside time, like she exists across time, and I remember Ruth saying that the painting had buds and open flowers and that was to show the flower in all its stages and that each and every bloom was complete with everything already inside it.

"Jess?" I look over at Cass; she's looking at me, puzzled. "You okay?" she asks. I nod and suddenly I want to cry, and it's because she's so beautiful, and I don't know why they did this. How they thought that they could fix things in the future, how they thought there was any sense of coming back from this. If they couldn't reignite the song in the throat of a bird, how on earth did they think they could put someone like Cass back together?

"Jess? What's wrong?" she asks.

"It's just the blossoms," I say, my voice breaking. "There was a man that used to paint them, they were his absolute favorite thing to paint."

Cass smiles. "I can see why," she says, but her smile is fading and she's looking at my face in worry.

"When he was ill, he would try to get better just so that he could come back and paint them."

"That's a lovely thing," she says, still studying me.

"Yes," I say. "I suppose so."

She looks over, wipes her brow with her hand, and gets back to brushing.

♣ ♣ ♣ ♣

Tonight there's less food, the protest now long forgotten. Cass and I share what we get, and we walk around the exercise yard arm in arm. We can hear Charmian laughing and I swear it grows louder the more authority she has.

"It was kind of you to apologize to her," Cass says. "I don't think she would be so fair to you."

"I was wrong. I blamed her, and I shouldn't have."

"You didn't have to apologize, but you did."

I don't know what to say.

"I almost hated her when they took Deva," says Cass.

"Almost?" I ask, smiling.

"Almost," she says. "I suppose some people are harder to like, it doesn't mean they're bad, though." She pauses a moment, and I know she's working up to saying something else.

"I haven't seen Eliot around for a while," she says, trying to make her voice sound artless, but failing miserably.

"No, he gets stationed in the city and then back here."

"He's nice."

"Yes, he is."

I know what she's thinking. "I don't love him, Cass." Her shoulders fall.

"We're not like you and Deva, he's just a friend."

"I'm a little disappointed," she says.

I roll my eyes. "Not everyone's a hopeless romantic, Cass."

"No, it's not that," she says. "It's just it would be nice if you opened up a little, had someone else to talk to too."

I feel slightly stung by that and she realizes it.

"I'm sorry," she says, and she stops walking, grabs my arms. "I didn't mean it like that, it's just, I care about you."

"I'm opening up, Cass. I have Eliot now, Zuri too. Emily. You've helped me see I need other people, I can't do everything myself."

She smiles, gives me a hug, and we start walking toward the entrance to the bunkhouse as we hear the bell ring, our skirts dragging in the dust.

"How much longer do you think we have to wait?" Cass asks quietly.

I keep walking. "We still haven't got the lighter, but we can't wait too long now we've got the dresses. If they search the bunkhouses, we're done for."

Cass leans in and we walk arm in arm back into the bunkhouse, take off our dresses, and lay them on our beds, then take our rags for washing. I line up again behind Cass and wait. We're the last today and the floor is wet. I listen as Cass throws the bowl of water over her feet, and then there's a pause. I look out at the darkness, watch as a sliver of moon appears in the sky, and start to frown.

"Cass?" I whisper. "Cass?"

I hear her moving, and she comes to the screen, her face ashen, her eyes luminous with tears. I look at her, confused, and notice that there's a smudge of blood on her thigh. She tries to tell me, but I just grab her, hold her.

"It's happening," she says. "It's happening."

35.

"Mum?! Mum!"

The house looks exactly same, the same gray walls, the same burned grass in the front, and Eliot tells me to get out, and I hitch up my blue dress, and I run up the path toward the door. The heat is brutal, I can feel it on the back of my head, but I keep running, and there's this strange silence all around. The door is unlocked, and I push it open with my hand, and I can hear someone.

"Mum?! Mum!"

I stop in the hallway but all I can hear is my own breathing. "Mum! Mum!"

And there's this gasp, this strange noise, and a chair moving, and then I'm sure I can see her in the living room and I run toward her but she's not there and the house looks different and I run to each of the rooms and push the doors open and all that's there are the posters we put up, ripped off the walls and thrown on the floor, and then I hear a voice and I turn. . . .

"Jess? Jess!" and I turn around and there she is and I run toward her and she wraps her arms around me and I feel like I've never been away and she holds the sides of my face like she can't believe it and she kisses me, kisses me, and I'm crying and then I hear another voice and it's Ruth.

"Is that you?" and she comes into the front door behind me and Mum looks at me and she says, "Shey is here, he's here, he was allowed to come home," and I run into the living room and there he is, looking older, a bit more like a man, but it's Shey and I run to him and just as he opens his arms, I wake in a sweat and my heart is pounding. I roll over, grab the sides of my bunk, try to breathe. It's quiet, no sound except the wind outside. I try to steady my breath, I'm here, I'm okay. I look at the lines of the floor, concentrate, and I feel my heart begin to slow down. I roll onto my back, look up at Cass, see the outline of the knife. My back is soaked in sweat, cooling now against the sheet.

Last night I came back to the bunk to fetch the knife, cut part of my washrag into strips, pushed them under my vest, and walked with them over to Cass. We washed out her underwear, agreed that we'd hide it until we can get away. We'll have to get away. Cass was shaking, and I couldn't get her to stop, and I was so angry that something so normal, so natural, was scaring her so much, and then we heard Mother Clement come in, so I went back to the bunk, leaving her to walk on her own in case we drew attention. She came back after a while and curled up on the bunk above. She's sleeping now, and I can't stop this restlessness, thoughts of Willow and mouth swabs and matches running through my mind.

They didn't match girls at first, perhaps they thought that it would cause upset, so they let the girls leave here at sixteen and have children with whomever they chose. Then, as things got worse, they brought the measure in, and Mum said they published all these papers saying that love was just science, chemistry and hormones, and they had worked it all out. All the stages of attraction and scent and then desire and dependency, and they said that love wasn't actually real, that it was just a mix of things that happened in your body that created a need, exactly like the need for sleep or food, and I could never understand it, because you can separate a painting into all the different colors and I could write them down in a list but that wouldn't explain why you look at a painting and cry. If you take apart a butterfly and examine all the different parts, you still can't put it back together or understand why it chose a particular flower, and it still doesn't explain why Ruth said that bees fall in love with a certain kind of flower sometimes and visit it over and over again and get to know the shape of it, the scent of it, and fly past all the other flowers just to get to it.

 Shey loves science and I am kind of glad that he does, because except for that book about drawing, it means we never fought over books. He loved to find out how stuff worked and how wonderful science was before the bees went, how much potential it had, and then after everything fell apart, he would sit and think of ways that the world could be started again as if he could solve it like a problem. He told me once of these seed banks that people kept in case of a disaster, where they took samples of seeds from every plant in the world and stored them so that habitats could be resuscitated, but they'd kind of forgotten that once the world changed, once climates changed, then the seeds couldn't survive anyway. And then he'd think about how he could try to cool the world, and when he was around nine, he'd draw these machines over and over again, and Mum would look at them and make these encouraging sounds, but then, over the years, he kind of stopped, and I remember finding a box of his drawings once, and it was a shock because I had forgotten he'd done that, and it was a worse shock because I then remembered that he'd given up.

I turn over, look out at the dark. He said once that they had never been able to prove the existence of love, and I remember thinking about it. That they could measure your hormones, that they could test your genes so that you could have a "healthy" baby, whatever that meant, but despite looking and looking, they could not find love. They wanted to isolate it, skewer it on a pin, or slice it and place it on a cold slide in a microscope so that they could examine it, and I want to laugh and cry at the same time because of how irrational humans are. The way we wanted to test this thing that is a billion colors, most of which we cannot see. They wanted to know it, when its whole purpose is to be unknown. They tried to put themselves at the center of something that does not have a center and the only way to see it is to snatch glimpses of it throughout your life as we blaze into darkness like falling stars. I have seen it, though, in Cass's face, in Zuri. I've seen it in the blue sky above the trees and the shards of light that fall on our heads. I've heard it in Eliot's voice when he talks about his father, and I've felt it when I've painted. I know it's real.

It's getting light now, and we'll have to get up soon. I suppose they needed proof to force girls to marry, so they made proof, they made evidence of what they were looking for. They packaged it up tidily and sold it to everyone, but I can't stop thinking of Cass and Deva, and of Mum and Dad, the affectionate way she still talks about their messy, imperfect marriage and the colors in how she loved him.

36.

Cass has gotten up really early. I open my eyes and she's not there; she's probably gone to change. I lie in bed a moment, listen as the girls begin to wake around me. Cass comes back and pulls on her dress quickly and sits on the floor. I push myself up on my elbow, every muscle aching from sleeping so tensely. I drop my feet to the floor, Cass's back between my knees, and I start to rake my fingers through her hair.

"We'll have to do yours soon," she says, and I think about how my hair has grown, how short it was, and how long that means I've been here. I don't say anything but start to plait her hair and then she rests her cheek on my hand, and I lean over and kiss her head. We stay there a moment until the door opens and a guard comes in. We all know what this means.

It's the usual guard—blond, young looking. He doesn't carry anything with him—there's no point for the information to be given in writing as most of the girls can't read, and the guards can't either. They memorize the names and recite them. I watch as Mother Clement follows him in.

"Anaisha Singh, you have been matched with Connor Mckensey."

Everyone goes quiet when names are called. Those still sitting on the floor having their hair plaited kind of bow their heads, those doing the braiding slow down to listen, and those in the wash queue turn around. Charmian has come to lean on the doorframe and listen, a certain confidence about her, the kind of look that suggests that she's waiting for something, wants to witness something.

"Rose Edwards, you have been matched with William Davies."

I don't know Rose, and I look around, wondering which one she is, as I carry on tying the string on the end of Cass's hair.

"Evelyn Price, you have been matched with Calvin James." Cass gets to her feet and sits on the bunk beside me.

"Charmian Green . . ."

A surprised murmur goes up and Cass's eyes snap over to me. Charmian gives a knowing smile.

"Charmian Green, you have been matched with Stephen Donnelley." It's like switching off a light, Charmian's face. Her smile drops and she seems completely lost. I watch as she stands up straight.

"What?"

The guard looks over at her, astonished. No one ever questions him. "Charmian Green, you've been matched with Stephen Donnelley."

She laughs, much to the guard's irritation. "No, you've got that wrong."

"Charmian, watch yourself." It's Mother Clement now, getting up from her chair.

"But he's got it wrong," Charmian insists.

The guard looks incensed. "You'll be married in the next few days."

"I am not marrying Stephen Donnelley," Charmian says, moving toward the guard. His face hardens dangerously, and as he turns to walk out, I feel Cass's hand on my arm.

Charmian's hurrying after him now. "You've got it wrong," she shouts, pure desperation in her voice, and as she touches his arm, he swings around and slaps her across the face. It happens so quickly. Charmian falls to her knees. Cass winces and buries her head in my side. I feel ill.

The guard is almost at the door now, but Charmian gets up and races toward him again, her voice getting higher and more on edge.

"You've got it wrong, you idiot! You have to check."

She grabs onto his arm again, but this time the guard continues walking so she's dragged along behind him, through the doorway and into the yard. Her friends are completely quiet. I don't want to think about what'll happen to Charmian, and I'm willing her, willing her to let him go.

We move over to the windows, and we can still hear her. "Listen to me!" she's shouting. "LISTEN!"

At this the guard turns again, grabs her by the hair. They're almost at the gate now and we watch as he drags her through with him. The girls are gasping, even Mother Clement looks away, and I feel this icy-cold dread, a sensation that I can describe only as complete terror.

♣ ♣ ♣ ♣

Cass is taken to brush, and Zuri, Emily, and I go to the Brush House, but we can hardly look at one another. Eliot is not there, only the new guards, and today the glue smell makes me sick. The hair on the table makes me sicker, and knowing that Charmian's will soon be there is even worse. We work slowly today even though the younger guard is chiding us. I go over to wash my hands, and he follows me.

"Your friend's not here," he spits. I notice how bad his teeth are.

"I'm sorry, I don't know who you're talking about."

"Your friend O'Brien."

He has these dangerous eyes, they don't settle, they shine with this restlessness. "I don't know O'Brien," I say as I rub the gel into my fingers.

He watches me and I know enough by now not to show anything. "I don't trust him," he says matter-of-factly.

"Why not?" I ask.

"Something about him," he says. "I just wanted you to know that." I frown, know what he's doing.

"Thanks for letting me know," I say in my politest voice, and I'm moving to walk past him when he steps into my path. He's smiling at me now and I stare straight into his chest, waiting patiently for him to move out of my way. At last he does, and I walk back to the workstation as calmly as I can and pick up another brush handle. I wind the string around and around, my eyes finding Zuri every now and again. We can't get near the lighter, and at the end of the day we line up to walk back to the bunkhouse. It's quiet until the trucks return and the girls flood back in, exhausted, hot, irritable.

Cass comes back and disappears once again to wash. I wait for her, and we walk to eat together.

"Was Eliot out on the trees today?" I ask.

She shakes her head. "Why?" she asks.

I shrug. "Nothing." I try to rationalize, he's moved around so much, it's just that the guard was dangerous, I could feel it. The food is put on our trays, we take our vitamins, and then we walk to find a table and try to eat, although neither of us has much of an appetite. We don't talk much either, the image of Charmian being dragged away looming large in our thoughts.

"It was so horrible," whispers Cass, as if reading my mind. I put down the bread in my hands. "I was thinking maybe she's in love with someone," she offers.

I shrug. "There's something, definitely something."

"A guard? That's what some of the girls were saying, anyway." It was the way Charmian's face changed, her disbelief, that was scary. You could tell that she had absolute faith in something and in that moment it had shattered. The depth of her disbelief showing the strength of her conviction. "There's this one who always comes to get her."

I think of the night I saw her laughing with the guard, the things she always had to trade. "We'll find out what's going on eventually," I say, and push the tray away from me.

When we get back to the bunkhouse, the girls are all talking about Charmian, their faces animated, and I feel even sicker. Cass goes to wash, and I make my way to my bunk, take off my dress, and sit there, and that's when Charmian comes in, and everyone goes quiet, and my heart skips a beat on seeing her. She's pale, her eyes vacant, there's a terrifying stillness to her, and there's a dark mark on the side of her face, a smudge of blood at the corner of her mouth. I get up instinctively, not because I want to look at her, but because I'm shocked to see her. She doesn't smile, she doesn't even look around, she walks to her bunk quietly, submissively, and that scares me more than anything.

37.

We're standing farther back in the Assembly Hall today. The longer we're here, the farther back we get, and the younger girls stand in front of us. Cass was pacing all morning, and I had to hold her hand, pull her to sit on the bunk so she could calm down. I was nervous too as she had something of Shey about her, an honesty that under scrutiny would just crumble. No one else knows she started her period and I told her to pretend to herself that nothing is different, that nothing happened, and she has to believe it in every cell of her body, that is the only way. She did well on the way over and now she's standing close to me, her arm against mine. The doors close and the guards take their places.

Father Renatus makes us wait again today, all part of the performance, a trick designed to make us feel that we are in all ways secondary, and when he does appear, he seems calmer than usual, his collar undone, a sense of ease. He walks to the lectern and pauses, knowing that he's building anticipation. After the oath, he looks out at us.

"I'm pleased to say that all of the brushing has been completed for this year."

There is a gasp at this, and I feel suddenly irritated by the fact that this is seen as progress or an achievement.

"From now until next year we will concentrate on the greenhouses."

A hum goes around the hall at this.

"The work you have done has been meaningful, has given us fruit that we have been able to trade in order to keep you safe and fed...."

I look at the floor.

"I know it has not been an easy time. The heat, the hours, the physical labor, but you must remember that there is a system, and we must all follow it in order to survive."

I feel Cass reach for my hand, squeeze my fingers.

"I am glad that you have come to your senses and have seen how much you are valued." His eyes sweep the hall and rest on the younger girls in front.

"I am glad that you can see a future here for each and every one of you. Let us put all that"—he pauses—"recent unpleasantness behind us and move on to the future as the community and as the family we are."

Silence. There's an edge to it, a strange weight behind it, and even though there is no noise at all, you can feel the resistance in it, and Father Renatus is clever enough to want to move things along. His eyes snap to the side of the stage.

"To celebrate, we have the latest girls who will be leaving us to start new lives and new families. Please welcome them."

He begins to clap, moving to the side so the girls in blue can climb up the stairs, but no one joins in. Not even the girls standing by the guards, or the youngest ones, who were most eager to please.

"I said, please welcome them." At this some of the guards join in and his face straightens, his fake smile hardens, and he knows that he cannot keep clapping as it is highlighting his lack of control. I feel the hair on the back of my neck bristle. He stops and we look and on the stage are eleven girls. Some I don't know; some I recognize, and then there's Charmian. Her face looks pale against the blue dress. Sickly. My heart sinks and I feel Cass tighten her grip on my fingers. "Rose Edwards, please . . ."

A dark-haired girl moves forward and Mother Jackson gestures to the wooden chair. Rose looks frightened as she sits. Mother Jackson takes the scissors from her apron and gathers Rose's hair into a ponytail and then she begins to cut. We expect Father Renatus to start clapping, but he doesn't, and because it's so quiet, all we can hear is the snagging of the blunt blade in her thick hair. Mother Jackson hacks away until she has a handful of Rose's hair. Rose is crying loudly.

"Be quiet!" he snaps, and Rose presses her palms to her face.

Then Rose gets up and another girl sits. Rose goes to stand at the edge of the stage and Father Renatus watches as the new girl gets her hair cut to just below her ear line. He looks pleased, in control, and his pleasure kind of reverberates through his frame, and I am mesmerized by his addiction to power, his pathetic craving for it. Yet with every girl that sits, he seems in my eyes to shrink, his insatiable appetite for control making him smaller.

I feel Cass tug at my sleeve to draw my attention to Charmian as she stands in line. She's watching Father Renatus, she's studying him, and I don't know what she's going to do. It's like she's expecting him to do something, but he doesn't, and then there's a young-looking girl getting her hair cut and the scissors seem to be getting blunter and blunter until the girl is sobbing as the hacking hurts so much and Mother Jackson becomes more and more frantic and then eventually there's only Charmian left. Father Renatus turns his attention to her as the other girls cry in the background. She looks at him, and for a moment it feels like he's about to speak to her, but then he gestures to the seat. Charmian stands, studies his face, and then her eyes are drawn to the chair, and she begins to walk over, hesitantly taking a seat. She's still looking at him, though, puzzled, as if she doesn't quite know what's happening despite having seen this ritual many, many times. She sits and Mother Jackson is starting to gather up her hair when he begins to speak.

"I'll do this one," he says as if he doesn't know her name.

Charmian looks up, Mother Jackson looks confused. He moves toward Mother Jackson and dismisses her with a gesture. He takes the scissors from her and goes to stand behind Charmian. Charmian's eyes are flickering everywhere, and she looks like she's about to cry, and then he rests his hands on her shoulders, palms down.

"Everyone has their role to play," he says calmly, and there's something about the way his forefinger is touching her neck that makes me understand that this is not the first time he has touched her.

"Our job is to be useful."

Charmian is staring forward now, her eyes glazed over. He's looking down at her and there's this triumph in his gaze and I feel tears spring to my eyes. He's squeezing her skin with his white fingers now, pinching it, kneading it almost, and this is not about brushing. "And when we are no longer useful, we move on to be useful to others."

I gasp, and Cass looks at me, bewildered. This is about those things that men take. "Now, there's a good girl."

This is about humiliating her.

He gathers up Charmian's hair and twists it tightly so that it becomes easier to cut. He pulls her head backward sharply and begins to tear at her hair with the blunt blades. I watch, my heart in my mouth as silent tears fall on her face and mine.

38.

There's a silence inside me now. It was here when I walked to the Brush House, and it was here when I had to stop and be sick on the way, and as Mother Clement watched me impatiently, and it was here when Emily and Zuri were looking at me and trying to catch my eye. I feel it, that silence that comes when I know something is about to happen. It's like my mind knows it needs to be sharp. I pick up the handles and I pinch the hair and I wind the strings and all the time my mind is homed in on the small plastic lighter that's behind me, and even though I can't see it, I know its exact position, its color, and I look at Zuri and she knows and I know without either of us having to say anything.

The young guard is walking in circles around us again, and every now and then, he stops by us in the same petty show of power that he has learned from those teaching him, and then he goes on his way. It will be a shorter day today as we had Assembly this morning and Mother Clement has already left, so there's one less pair of eyes watching us.

The thing is, I'm not afraid anymore, now that their power seems so petty. Those who are supposed to know, to guide, to show the way, are no more than children with their petty squabbles and their need to feed their egos, to destroy everything and anything to get what they want. I know that they haven't learned anything, and Mum used to say that it was part of our pattern, like the tides. How we live in ease and then create hardship and then wish for the tide to come in again, how we create the same cycles over and over until something or someone comes along and breaks them. And we did break them, we broke them when we did not stop to listen, and now, in the mess, we're back to our old patterns again, but there must be those who see that? There must be those who want to create new ones. Perhaps the only way forward is to burn everything down. I think and think, look at the brushes in front of me, and then I walk over to get more handles, and a girl called Natalie hands me some.

"Is that all you've done?" I ask her sharply. She looks up at me in shock and the young guard spins around.

"Be quiet!" he hisses.

"She's too slow," I say, and Emily looks over and suddenly her face changes as she begins to understand. Natalie looks at me in disbelief as I walk away.

"Back to work!" the guard snaps.

I work faster now, trying to get through as many brushes as I can, and Zuri matches my pace. I feel sorry for Natalie, but it's the only way. We work for another hour or two until the brush handles are finished once again, and I walk back toward Natalie, and the guard follows me over.

I make a show of waiting impatiently as she strips more wood, and the guard becomes interested in her lack of progress. I wait and take as many handles as I can, and she looks at me, hurt. He stays with her, chiding her to speed up. Zuri looks over at me and we work as quickly as we can for another hour as I can tell that the sun is already moving to the other side of the building.

It's getting warmer, as it always does at this time of day, and I can see the sweat on Zuri's cheeks under her eyes, I can feel it under my armpits and then I look at her and I walk to wash my hands and I hope it's enough. Zuri walks toward Natalie, and I take some gel and rub it on my skin.

"There's still no more?" asks Zuri.

"She's so slow," says Emily, and suddenly Natalie shoves Zuri in the chest and the guard comes between them and I take my chance and my hand is on the lighter and I slip it into my apron and I walk back and grab Zuri as if afraid that she is going to retaliate. The guard raises his hand to Natalie, and then, thankfully, he stops.

"Get back to work!" he screeches, and his voice is broken and high and he sounds like nothing more than what he is: a young child afraid of losing control. Natalie stares at Zuri and Emily with angry tears in her eyes and I try not to show the remorse I'm feeling. We work for another hour, not even raising our eyes to one another in case anything shows in our faces. At the end of the day, Zuri shuts off the stove and washes her hands, blocking the view of the guards from the door. She makes her way toward me, and I place a hand on her shoulder, start to follow her back to the bunkhouse, keeping the lighter protected between us.

The other girls have been in the bunkhouse all day—the greenhouses are not open yet—and they are hot, argumentative. The air is thick with a deep unease. There's whispering everywhere. A sense that something has changed, that something unseen is coming to light. I move to sit on my bunk and Cass slips down to sit by my side, and we both look out the window, try to block the sound around us. I put my hand into my apron, hold the lighter, and conceal it in my hand before lifting my arm and pushing it underneath Cass's mattress. She looks at me and understands, her eyes wide.

Although it's not time to eat yet, it is already getting darker. There's an eerie blueness to the sky and the wind is picking up, blowing the occasional blossom petal across the exercise yard so that it looks like I imagine snow appears.

There are truck lights outside the perimeter fence as they bring the brides to collect their meager belongings so that they can be transferred to their husbands for the journey out of camp. I cannot speak, and I feel Cass lay her head on my shoulder, and all of a sudden we hear the gates of the exercise yard open, and I look up to see the brides walking in a line toward the bunkhouses, their dresses luminous in the gloaming, the skirts blowing to the side in the breeze as they separate off to their respective bunkhouses. It's getting dark in here now too, but instead of settling down, there's a preoccupied hum among the girls as they huddle together in groups talking. Cass and I sit in the stifling gloom, guards standing at the still-open gates, and all I can see are more petals drifting in across the yard, and I get up and walk to the doorway of the bunkhouse and stand looking out at the strange blizzard, and then I hear her voice behind me.

"I wanted to give you these."

I turn. It's Charmian, her voice small. "Give them back to Cass, will you?"

She passes me the box of dominoes and I notice that her hands are trembling. I take them, hold on to them.

She looks so young with her short hair, that bruise they gave her darkening on her face. We stand in silence a moment.

"You know I always listened to Cass and Deva. How they'd argue whether dominoes was a game of luck or strategy. I guess I wanted to find out."

She looks tired. So tired. "And which was it?" I ask.

She smiles sadly. "I tried strategy," she says, and begins to say something else but the words get stuck in her throat. "Guess I lost."

There are these large, slow tears forming in her eyes now and I want to reach out to her. She looks away, out to the darkness for a moment, a tear rolling down her cheek.

"He said he loved me."

She kind of throws down the words, lets them out from this dark place inside her and into the light. "How stupid was I?"

I shake my head. "You're not stupid, he manipulated you. It wasn't your fault."

She looks back at me, laughs bitterly through her tears. Nods. "You know, me and you could've been friends," she says again.

"We still can be," I offer, but she shakes her head now and

frowns and then she takes my free hand and places it on her stomach and suddenly my blood runs cold.

"They'll never let me get rid of it," she confides, her voice breaking.

She lets go of my hand, wipes her tears away. "You were the artist, right?"

I stare at her. She looks pale, her eyes sunken. I nod. She nods too.

"I knew you were." She pauses. "I almost told them, but something held me back. I guess I knew on some level I respected what you were doing. And you understood things I didn't," she whispers. "Well, not at first, anyway. That open door . . ."

She smiles sadly. "It was beautiful." My throat is burning with tears.

She looks me square in the eyes now.

"Get out of here if you can, Jess," she says, and there's a strange intimacy in the way she says my name, and then she does something I wasn't expecting. She leans across and she kisses my cheek, and my skin is wet from her tears, and we stay like that for a little while. Then she steps back, straightens her spine, steadies herself.

"I have to go," she says, and starts to move past me. "I'll walk with you," I find myself saying.

"You don't have to. . . ."

"I'd like to."

She looks a little bewildered at first, then she smiles, waits as I put down the dominoes, and takes my hand, and we walk out into the gloaming as the girls begin to follow us out and gather around. We fall into step together, the dust at our feet like any two girls in the history of the world walking arm in arm as if they were on their way to school or across a park. And then I feel her slow down, and we come to a stop in the middle of the exercise yard. She turns to me and takes both my hands.

"They won't break me," she whispers. "They think they have, but they won't get their way." Her voice is flinty and suddenly there's a look on her face that scares me. She smiles at me and there's this flash of the old Charmian there, the sneer, the superiority. She lets go of my hands and starts to speak.

"My name is Charmian Green!" she shouts. The guards all turn to look at her. "And I've been matched with Stephen Donnelley."

The guards begin to walk toward us now and the Mothers turn their heads to listen. The girls encircle us, and Charmian takes control again. She looks flushed now, her eyes shining, and suddenly she's back in charge and I cannot breathe.

"They want me to marry Stephen Donnelley because I am pregnant."

She laughs now and the exercise yard begins to fill with a murmur, a hum that is growing.

"I am *with child*." Her voice is mocking. She's reckless, undaunted. "I didn't even have my first period. Wasn't even allowed to become a woman."

"Quiet!" a guard shouts, and a gunshot rings out into the air. I flinch, but Charmian does not. "Quiet?" she says.

"You like us to be quiet!" she shouts again. "But we won't be! Not anymore."

Another shot rings out, and Charmian laughs this carefree laugh that even bullets can't silence. "Because the child is not Stephen Donnelley's, it is Father Renatus's. He put it there by tricking me, by lying to me, by making me feel like nothing...." Another shot, and Charmian turns now, her eyes dancing across the faces around us, and I can hear her breathing heavily.

"And they want me to pretend that it is Stephen Donnelley's to spare Father Renatus the shame, the nuisance, and then he will choose another girl and the cycle will go on! This is who we brush for, this is who we give our lives to!" she shouts.

There's a commotion as the Mothers start to move toward us, but astonishingly, the girls hold them back.

"His shame is not my shame!" Her voice is hoarse now. "I will not lie!" she screams defiantly, and then more quietly, "And I will not stay here." She's sobbing now. "I will have my freedom! You will not take away my freedom. I am free to do as *I* wish!"

All eyes are on her and there's this pause as if the guards and the Mothers don't know what to do, and then she begins to walk away toward the open gate.

"Charmian!" I say. "Charmian!" But she doesn't turn, and all I can see is her dress that is this cerulean blue as she begins to walk toward the entrance to the exercise yard, and the whole sky above us is filled with luminous petals, a wild snowstorm of blossoms.

"Stop! First warning!" shouts a guard.

"Charmian, stop!" I say, taking a few steps toward her, but she's walking away, and she knows exactly what she's doing.

She doesn't break stride as she steps toward the perimeter, her short, wavy hair blowing in the wind, her whole figure confident and assured.

"Stop! This is your second warning!" The guard has the gun on his shoulder now.

"Charmian, please!" I can hear only my heart pounding and the wind howling, but she keeps on walking, her head held high.

"Stop! Final warning!" the guard screams, his voice reverberating around us.

As the gunshot rings out, filling the world around me, everything seems to slow down. A crimson mark blooms on the back of her dress.

"CHARMIAN!" I run toward her.

She seems to fall to the ground slowly as if she is floating through water. I reach out for her as the folds of her dress undulate around her until her body shudders to stillness on the sterile earth.

There's no sound, there's nothing. I drop to my knees as a pool of dark blood spreads underneath her. Her face is still, her cheek on the ground, a dark curl on her temple, and as I reach out, touch her face, my hand trembling, I hear a sound, and it's coming from me and it sounds like anguish, like fear, like rage. I take my hand back, and there's blood on it, and I look over my shoulder through the storm of petals to see the bunkhouses on fire.

39.

I feel an arm under my elbow, dragging me to my feet. There's a voice. "Jess, get up!" I can't focus.

"Jess, come on!" And suddenly I find Zuri's face in my line of sight. She has her palm on the side of my face, her eyes blazing.

"Jess, look at me! Look at me!" I try to bring her into focus, her face inches away from mine. "Come on, it's time, we've got to go." She shakes me by the arms, and I stumble to my feet, and there's smoke catching at the back of my throat. The girls have started running toward the open gateway and there are more gunshots.

"We'll get killed," I say breathlessly. There's a girl on her knees to our right, she's injured, bleeding.

"Now's our chance, they can't shoot us all," Zuri says.

"Where's Cass?" I ask.

"She's coming with Emily."

Zuri steadies me as we're jostled away. There's a crush of girls trying to get through the open gate and beyond them are guards shouting at one another, some of them backing away, looking at one another in panic. I grab on to Zuri's hand, afraid to let her go, and there's this surge, this pressure, some of the girls pressed up against the fence, and the guards look as young and inexperienced as the girls they're watching, and then suddenly, an older guard comes from somewhere, starts to shout.

"Let them through! There's a fire! Let them through!"

"We need to stay here, in the middle," Zuri says as we push forward. There are hundreds of girls in the yard now, and the guards relent and begin to open another gate. There's more shouting now as tens of girls surge forward, and I can feel Zuri's fingers slip away from mine.

"Zuri!" I gasp. "Zuri!"

I can't breathe, it's like there's no air.

"Jess!" I look up and there's just the sky and smoke and petals and I can feel the life being squeezed out of me, tighter, tighter, and everything goes small and far away for a moment, and I think, *Don't let me die here, don't let me have come this far.* And then there's this release, an exhalation as the girls get through and out into the camp and I'm kind of carried forward with everyone else until I'm dropped as the girls space out, and I fall to my knees, and I'm coughing. I try to steady my breathing, steady it, and I stagger to my feet again and turn around, look backward, and it almost takes my breath away again. There's smoke, and this endless movement, and then there are these clear, defined orange flames flickering in the roofs of the bunkhouses. I turn, look for Zuri, scan the faces, their hollow eyes lit up by the glow of the flames.

"Zuri!" I shout, coughing. "Zuri!"

"Jess!"

And then I see her running toward me through the crowd and the guards are getting the last of the girls out of the exercise yard and I look around for Cass and Emily but they're nowhere to be seen.

"We need to find Eliot," Zuri says.

"He said he'd bring a truck," I gasp. "We have to wait for Cass and Emily, they can't be far behind."

"They stayed behind to light the fires. They'll be last out."

"Then we'll wait."

And then there are gunshots as all the girls start marching for the main headquarters and the gateway beyond, and suddenly a young girl runs straight into me, and I look down and it's her. The little girl I always see, and her eyes are wide, and I grab her arms, both of them.

"Run, okay?" I say. "Just get away from here."

She nods and she tears herself away and an older girl grabs her hand, nods at me, and pulls her after her. Zuri grabs my arms and we hunker down by the side of a nearby army truck. I scan faces, look at the throng of bodies, of girls.

"He's over there!" says Zuri, yanking my arm, her voice breathless.

I try to follow her line of sight and it's him—Eliot. The guard from the Brush House is by his side with a gun on his shoulder. Zuri starts to get up, but I pull her back.

"The other guard'll kill you."

She nods and I look back around the side of the truck again, search the faces, look for the red hair, and for Emily's serious face.

Suddenly there are two feet in front of me and I look up,

like I did that first day, and it's Cass, Emily by her side. Cass is breathing heavily, clutching a pillowcase to her stomach, and I pull her down, grab on to her neck tight.

"We did it," she says under her breath. "We lit the fires."

She throws her head back and I stare at her. She looks wild, like she cannot believe this, and she looks like she's grown, like a woman. And then there are more gunshots.

"We need to wait until the other guard is gone before we can get to Eliot's truck," I whisper, and she nods and then she slips the knife to me, and even among the panic it's searingly cold in my hand. We both look at it a moment, and then I think.

"Turn around," I say. Cass looks at me, looks at the knife, and she knows.

She sits, hunkers between my legs, and I gather up her hair—her beautiful hair the color of fire, the hair I've spent hours untangling and plaiting—and I begin to cut it with the knife. Through the waves, the length, the glossiness, I cut it off, the blade of the knife making easy work of it, and then Cass turns, looks at the hair in my hand, and I've never seen her look more alive, her face aglow. I give her the knife, turn my head, and she cuts mine, amid the screaming girls and the smoke, and I feel the weight of it lift, the length that had grown back over the last months.

"They're fighting," says Zuri suddenly, and I look across. The guard has Eliot up against the truck and Eliot's gun on the floor.

"Cut your hair, Emily's too," I say to Zuri, handing her the knife. She nods and follows my eyes across to Eliot. "We're running out of time," I say, and start to get up when there's another gunshot, and then Eliot is on his knees. I look over in panic and he's clutching his arm, the guard standing over him. I'm up now, ready to run.

"What are you doing?" It's Cass. "Jess? What are you doing?!"

I don't know what I'm doing, maybe that's the truth, but I can't stay here and I start running toward Eliot and the guard and he's still shouting at Eliot and then suddenly he sees me and he spins around, infuriated, and I stop. Then I walk slowly, so slowly, and I try to remind myself that he's just a kid, even though he's trying to make himself look like a man. "Get back!" he shouts, and I can see the whites of his eyes. "Get back, I said!"

I have the knife hidden in my hand, and I don't really know what I'm doing, but it's not like I've gone outside of myself. For the first time in my life, it feels like I *am* myself, and then I get closer and closer, and he puts the gun on his shoulder, and he takes aim at me, his arm shaking, his hand trembling, and I just walk, because he's just a young boy and he's trying to pull the trigger, but he can't, and I keep looking him in the eye, and suddenly I'm only a few feet away from him and I stand and I look at him and he pulls down the gun from his shoulder and his breathing is heavy, and he's got this confusion on his face like he doesn't understand. I hadn't seen Eliot stumble to his feet, grab his gun, but when he has, he hits the guard over the head so he lands on the ground with a sickening thud. Eliot and I stand, both of us looking down at the guard, and then he looks up at me. Nods. "We've got to go," he says, wincing. He's bleeding through his jacket.

I look at him. "Are you okay?"

"I'll be all right. Come on!"

Zuri's behind me again and Emily grabs my arm, pulls me into the truck and Cass gets in the front and we hunker down as Eliot speeds away, driving with one arm. I see Cass in the front start to tug at the pillowcase, drag out the blue dresses, and as Eliot drives away, we pull them over our heads, just so they cover our work dresses.

"There's another coat under the seat," says Eliot, and Cass reaches for it and drapes it over Eliot's shoulders so that any guards won't be able to see the blood soaking through his sleeve. The first checkpoint waves us through, and for the first time since arriving here, we see the offices and Father Renatus's quarters. Cass stares. The guards have all filed off toward the exercise yard as the bells and the sirens blare. It's quiet, eerily silent as we drive toward the main gate. There are five or six guards. Eliot breathes deeply, I can see him try to focus. He slows down, tries to look nonchalant.

"I'm sorry, we're on lockdown," the guard says. "Something's happening in camp."

"I need to get these women through," replies Eliot, and if you didn't know him, you might not notice the strain in his voice.

"I'm sorry, we're not letting anyone through."

"They're married," replies Eliot. "I have their paperwork here. Surely you knew there were married girls going out today?"

The guard looks irritated. "I know, but we have our orders."

The other girls will be on their way here now.

I can't say anything, there's nothing I can do, I have to just sit here, keep quiet.

"You want to see the paperwork?" asks Eliot.

"No," the guard says defensively.

Eliot grabs some papers and shoves them through the open window toward him. He barely looks at them, and I suddenly realize why: he can't read.

"Their husbands are waiting for them, they're no longer residents here, they've been moved on," Eliot tries again. "I wouldn't want to be you if they get hurt in the riots."

I can see the guard begin to waver. Eliot pulls back the forms.

"You do know one of them is now married to a close friend of Colonel Porter? It says it right here." The young guard blanches at this, and suddenly Eliot begins to gain confidence.

"What's your name?" Eliot asks.

"What's that got to do with—"

"I need your name," Eliot says again. "I'm not going to be held responsible for this. I need your number too."

I try not to look at the guard's face as he calculates this risk in his mind.

"They're married?"

"Look at them," says Eliot, and the guard takes in our short hair, the blue dresses. "They're no longer supposed to be here...."

He looks back at us and I try to keep staring ahead, then he nods to his friends, and the gate opens. I can feel my heart pounding in my chest.

"At last," says Eliot impatiently as he starts the engine once again, and all I can hear is the scrape of the electric gate and the guard's radio crackling to life as someone on the other side begins to shout in a tinny voice, but they're too late as we drive away.

40.

Eliot drives fast along the back roads, all of us still silent. There are sirens blaring in the distance reminding us that we are not yet free. I look out, and there's this bare earth, and in the distance the shape of the city, and it's dark now, an orange haze above the tallest buildings, the sign of fire. There's a tense silence as we get nearer. I can't believe the number of people out on the streets. Eliot has to avoid the crowds, reverse, take alternative routes as every avenue in town is thronging with people, fires lit at the sides of the road. The atmosphere is electric. Dangerous. Eliot's looking pale now, even in the darkness I can see it. His breathing is shallow. I reach forward and put my arm on his shoulder.

"I'm okay," he says through gritted teeth. "It's been like this, the last few days. Something's changing, something big's happening."

Eliot follows my directions, and as we get nearer the house, I start to feel disoriented, and I can't figure out if it's because things have changed so much in so short a time or because I have. It's like everywhere looks familiar, but it's not. Eventually we find the road, and I grab on to Cass's seat in front of me as the house comes into view.

"Here," I say, and Eliot stops the truck. Zuri looks at me through the darkness and I can't breathe.

She squeezes my hand, and I get out, my legs weak, and make my way up the path. I hear the truck doors close behind me as the others follow. The path is the same, the worn grass is the same, the door a little more weathered, and I feel sick. So sick. I lift up my hand to knock and find myself not wanting to know what the answer will be, my hand hanging in the air. All those times I dreamed of being back here seem so far away now. I feel Cass's hand on my shoulder.

"You'll be okay," she says softly. I knock and we wait, and you can hear furniture being moved, voices. Unfamiliar voices.

"Who is it?" A man's booming voice. I look over at Cass.

"It's Jess," I say.

"Who?" He doesn't open the door.

"It's Jess!" I say, louder this time, and I hear the unmistakable metallic sound of a gun being loaded.

"It's okay!" I say, backing away a little. "I used to live here."

The door opens slightly, a sliver of a man's face appearing. He stares at me angrily. "Who the hell are you?"

"I'm sorry, I used to live here."

He looks at Cass, Zuri, Emily, the truck behind. "What's your business?"

"Nothing, I was . . . I was just looking for someone," I say.

"Well, get the hell away," he says, and slams the door shut. I stand, staring at the place that used to be home, until I feel Zuri pull at my hand.

"Jess? Come on, we tried."

I nod, tears in my eyes, then I think of Ruth.

"I need to try next door," I say. Zuri looks at Cass in concern, but I walk around the side of the house to the back where Ruth's door is. There's a small light on in one of the rooms, but the door is locked, barricaded probably. I knock lightly, but there's nothing, so I look at Cass and she helps me bang on the wood with her fists. Suddenly we hear the sound of movement.

"Hello?" comes a voice.

My heart leaps. "It's me! Ruth? It's me!"

We hear locks being undone, the sliding of bolts, and suddenly she's there, her white hair unbrushed, her clothes too baggy for her, and she looks at me with these watery eyes. She's small, frail, the sleeves of her cardigan baggy, and she just places her hand on the side of my face and starts sobbing. She throws her arms around me. I cry too, un-self-consciously, press my face into her familiar scent, her familiar hair, her familiar skin, and then she pulls away, takes in my face.

"I never thought I'd see you again, Anna," she says through her tears. I wipe my eyes, disbelieving, my relief short-lived.

"But it's me, it's Jess," I say, feeling suddenly weak. "Anna was—Anna is my mum." I smile, but I can feel my face crumpling.

She looks at me, frowning for a moment. "Of course she is!" she says. "Of course she is."

The house has changed; it is almost empty, and there's the smell of someone who hasn't washed for a while. There's nothing left of any value. Ruth takes my hand, walks me to the small sofa, and sits me down, looking at me all the while and stroking my hand.

"Where have you been all this time?" she asks.

I search her face. It's the same, only thinner, much thinner. Her eyes are the same too, the same kindness in the creases on her cheeks, the same gentleness in her smooth fingers. She has a small paraffin lamp lit, and it throws deep blue shadows around the shell of a room. Cass leads Eliot to sit on the sofa. Zuri sits down next to him, Cass on the floor.

"Ruth, I need to know where Mum is," I say, trying to mask the urgency in my voice. She looks at me with a sweet smile as if she hasn't heard me.

"Ruth?" I try again. "Do you know where Anna is?"

"She's not next door?" she asks.

"No," I say, my voice catching. "There's another family living there now."

She nods as if she knew this. "Of course. They help me sometimes."

I nod, my heart breaking. "What about Shey? You remember Shey?"

Her face brightens again. "He used to come and see your mother," she says. "Very smart in his uniform."

I look at Cass, my heart starting to beat faster.

"I haven't seen him for a while," Ruth says.

I don't know whether I want to ask any more, if I want to know any more.

"It is so lovely to see you," she says again. "You're staying awhile, aren't you? All of you?"

I look at her, not knowing what to say. Eliot shrugs. "If we stay tonight, we'll have to park the truck behind the house, get going early."

"We're going on a journey," I say, choosing my words carefully, "in the morning. A long journey through the border."

She seems to search her memory. "You'll have to be careful," she says. "They're not very nice on the border. I tried to cross it once." I choke on tears now, my words gone. All I can do is nod. I wait a moment, try to recover.

"Is there anything I can help you with?" she asks kindly.

"Do you have any medicine? My friend Eliot is hurt."

She looks confused. "Which one?"

"Me," he says, and I realize how weak his voice is. Ruth's face is suddenly serious. "Well, we better get you seen to," she says.

Zuri, Cass, and Emily lie on the sofa, trying to rest; they're exhausted, and before long, their breathing changes as they fall into a deep sleep. Ruth goes to find her medical kit and some fabric, which I hear her ripping into strips. I sit Eliot next to the lamp where the most light is. He throws off his jacket, the one slung over his shoulders, opens the buttons of the one underneath, but he can't shrug it off. He looks at me, and I offer to help but realize to my horror that the reason it's stuck is that the blood on the gunshot wound has dried, sticking the material to his skin. I try to be as gentle as I can, peel back the jacket, but he winces, grabs my hand, and stops me. His breathing is heavy, and I wait until he's ready. I get the jacket off and then unbutton his shirt, pull it over his shoulder. He's concentrating hard on the floor, trying to push away the pain, and suddenly I find myself humming, I don't know why. Perhaps it's because he said that the vibration of his father's guitar used to calm him, but I start humming so that this doesn't feel so painful, so bad. He looks up and tries to smile.

I listen as Ruth washes her hands, comes back with some boiled water, and looks at the wound. She presses on it, feels around it, trying to tell if there's a bullet still in there. She shakes her head.

"Flesh wound," she says, as if it were the most natural thing in the world, every old nursing instinct she ever had kicking in, dispelling any fears I had that she'd remember what to do. "I'll need to stitch it."

It is my turn to wince now as I watch her go and search for a needle.

"You okay?" he asks, his voice low.

I nod. "I think I should be asking you that."

He smiles. "I know you wanted to find your mother."

I find it difficult to look at him, anxious that if he sees the depths of my disappointment and fear, then I'll have to acknowledge them myself.

"We found Ruth, that's something," I say, trying to find something to cling to, to be grateful for.

I listen to him breathe a moment, his skin white in the lamplight. "Has she always been . . ." He tries to think of the words.

"She was having trouble with her memory when I left. Not this bad, though." I think. "Mum used to take care of her a lot. Help her out with food, routine, conversation. Looks like she's lost herself a little."

He nods. "I'm sorry," he says, and I have to bite my lip so as not to let my eyes fill with tears again.

Ruth brings back the sterilized needle and some thread and a brown bottle that she hands to Eliot. "Whiskey," she says. "It was my husband's. Drink it."

Eliot looks at her and I can see him weighing up his options, drink this or feel more pain. He unscrews the ancient bottle and takes a slug or two. Ruth and I wait until we notice his muscles relax a little, and then she pulls him closer to the light of the lamp and begins to stitch. I wait, pressing my palms over my ears as she works, trying to rationalize his pain, knowing that it has to be done. When she's finished, Ruth splashes some of the whiskey over the wound to sterilize it. He gasps, trying to control his breathing, and then he kind of just closes his eyes, and in a few moments, he's fast asleep. I stand up, hook my arms under his armpits, and tip him onto his side, let him lie on the floor. I take his jacket, fold it over a few times, and place it under his head. We both watch him for a moment, his face softening in sleep.

"He'll be all right, Jess," Ruth says. I look up at her in shock as she remembers my name. She gathers the medical kit together and takes it back to the kitchen. "And remind me to give you the letter your mother left you."

41.

I carry the paraffin lamp in one hand, run upstairs, and sit on Ruth's bed, my hands trembling. The letter is small, folded over a few times. It's written on the back of an old sketch of mine. It was in the cupboard under the stairs along with a box of supplies—medicines, maps, batteries. My heart is beating so fast, I can hardly breathe. Without even unfolding it, I know it's one of the drawings of the Pre-Raphaelite girls roaring with laughter, their eyes ablaze, challenging the viewer. I unfold it, try to push it into the small circle of light, narrow my eyes. It's been so long since I've read anything. It's definitely Mum's writing. It's hurried, that's for sure, but I would recognize it anywhere. I read hungrily, my hands trembling, my heart instinctively sinking at the shortness of the note. I scan the row of letters, my eyes scurrying across the page.

She's received a message from some of her friends, the ones she used to protest with, they're starting again, a new beginning. There's a valley somewhere, and there are these numbers that I assume are coordinates, and she says that they'll be free, and her heart is breaking because Ruth will not leave with her because she says she's too old and will slow them down. She has begged Ruth to come, but she wants to be at home, surrounded by her books. Mum can hardly write with the pain of leaving me behind, but she knows I'll make it. She's gathered some supplies, left them under the stairs for me, and she'll be there waiting for when I arrive. And she says that she loves me and is so proud of me and Shey and that he has come to see her a few times.

I push the tears from my eyes, frustrated that they're blurring my vision. I tip up the paper toward the light, try to make sense of it. She wants me to know that I made her happy, so happy, and let her see things she couldn't have seen alone, and she knows there's something better than this. *Come soon,* she says. *Come soon and I'll be waiting.* There's a date too, around three months ago, and I try to do the calculation: fourteen weeks, three days. Two thousand four hundred twenty-four hours. I turn the paper over, but that's it. There's nothing else. I turn it over once again and reread it from start to finish another ten, twenty times, my heart beating so hard, wanting to feel this new message from her in every part of my body and mind. Present. Here. Now.

I get up, look out the bars on the windows across the city and to the north. The tallest buildings are where the border is. Two thousand four hundred twenty-four hours ago she was here, that's all the time that has divided us, and perhaps I can find her in less than that. I refold the paper, press it to me, memorizing the coordinates, knowing I'll have to leave the letter behind in case we're searched at the border.

♣ ♣ ♣ ♣

I lie next to Ruth on her bed like I did sometimes when I was a little girl. I listen as she sleeps, and through the darkness, I see some familiar pictures. A bee I must have drawn her when I was younger. A pink flower, a pollen-covered bee, and those sketches of that apple, and as I stare at them through the semidarkness, slowly I feel my muscles start to relax, my mind drift, until I'm hardly conscious, but knowing that I am here, somewhere other than the camp. I fall into a deep and dreamless sleep.

I wake before dawn, feeling renewed. I rub my eyes, feel for the letter, and get up quietly. I walk around the bed, kiss Ruth's white hair, look at her sleeping, before making my way quietly downstairs. Eliot is stirring. He looks stiff, in pain, but he has a better color about him. I go to him, kneel down next to him, and show him the letter.

"It's from Mum," I say. "Ruth remembered she left it."

"What does it say?" he asks, frowning. I give him the paper.

"There are some coordinates. Years ago, she used to be friends with a group of rebels. She's found them again, and they've escaped north, where they're going to set up a new life, a new community. Start again. She wants us to go there."

"So, it was true, then? The story you told."

"Of course it was," I answer.

I can see his face become lighter, then he pulls me near, hugs me. He lets me go as the girls begin to stir. I go and wash my face as Zuri reads the letter to Cass and Emily, who both look unsure. I look in the kitchen with a new sense of energy, but there's nothing to eat really, and none of us want to take any of Ruth's meager rations. My heart aches for her, but it's best for all of us if we leave before she wakes. She might even think it was all a dream. I fill up a few old bottles with water and walk back to the living room.

"Mum's left us a ration box, a few things to barter."

"I took some ration packs, they're hidden in the truck," says Eliot. "You'll have to let me do the talking at the border. We'll just give them the paperwork, hope for the best." Zuri nods. "The earlier we go, the better—before they do a change-over."

Ruth has left Eliot a clean shirt, which must've belonged to her husband, and Eliot begins to pull it on, the collar much too large for him. I walk back toward him and help him on with his jacket, slowly, his arms stretched out so as not to hurt him. He nods when it's done, and I do up the buttons. I look up at him.

"It's best we go," I say, and he nods. I look around, reluctant to leave. The thought of leaving Ruth heartbreaking.

"We have to go," says Eliot.

We walk to the door, and I feel for Mum's letter, place it on the kitchen counter on the way out, and I catch Cass looking at it. Eliot walks out to the truck carrying the ration box, and Zuri and Emily follow him.

"Cass?"

She's still looking at the note.

"We have to go."

She looks at me and suddenly my heart sinks. Her eyes are full of tears.

"Cass? What's wrong?" My stomach jolts and I know; I

know what's coming. Her face crumples. "I can't leave Deva," she says simply.

I start shaking my head. "Cass, please, don't."

"I can't leave Deva. If she's here in the city as Eliot said, I have to find her."

I walk toward her, a panic rising in me. "Cass, we don't know where she is. She might be miles away by now!"

"What are you looking for, Jess?" she asks me unexpectedly, and her voice is steady.

I frown. "What do you mean?"

"What is it that you want? What are you running toward? Please, tell me."

I shrug. "A new start, a life, a future, freedom."

She nods now, heavy tears falling down her face. "So am I."

"But you . . ."

"And it's all in Deva."

"Cass, please . . ."

I can hear the truck outside, they're waiting.

"I have to find her," she says. "I'll look after Ruth awhile, search for Deva, and then we'll come find you."

"No. . . ."

"I want to do this."

"No. . . ."

"We'll come and find you," she says again.

I grab her arms, the thought of being without her unbearable. "Please, Cass," I beg.

"She's my freedom," she says, and I know, my heart sinking, that she's made up her mind. I clutch her to me, and I cannot breathe. She's crying too.

"I told you I'd stay with you as long as you needed me," she whispers. "You have so many people around you now, Jess. I need to do this. Please understand."

I hold her tight.

"I love you," she says, kissing the side of my face. "I love you so much." I pull away, try to etch her beautiful face into my mind.

"You've given me so much," she says. "I have never known anyone like you."

She's laughing now through her tears and both of us can hear Ruth stir upstairs.

"Now, go be free," Cass says, and she places the palm of her hand on my face. "Go be free, Jess."

42.

I try not to cry on the way to the border, try not to show my grief on my face. I swallow down the pain as Zuri sits by my side, Emily in front, all of us wordless. Eliot drives, keeping his face neutral, expressionless, in case we draw attention. The city gets busier as we get closer to the border, and up in front are rows of army trucks queuing.

The border is just how I remember it: there are barbed fences running the outline of the city and then several roads blocked off with barriers and booths bristling with soldiers. Eliot chooses a lane, knowing at some point that we will have to get out, show our paperwork, be questioned.

We wait, the sun rising above us. Our story is that we are wives being delivered to militia members stationed outside the border. The paperwork is in order, it will just depend on whether the soldiers will buy it and whether they will bother radioing to check. Eliot looks ahead, doesn't give anything away as we watch the vehicles in front being pulled in one by one, the drivers and passengers being questioned by impatient soldiers. It is warm today, really warm, and I can see Eliot shifting his weight uncomfortably in his jacket. We slow down as a solider waves us into a turnout.

"Get the paperwork ready, please," he says.

Eliot nods and we wait. There's an altercation between the soldiers in front of us and the security guard and it seems to take forever to resolve it. Everyone's on edge, the city incendiary, the border seemingly busier than usual, the soldiers tenser. Some soldiers walk past and look at Zuri and Emily and me. We're there for hours, the sun burning above us, the shadows moving across the road. Eliot is in pain, I can hear it in his breathing.

Then, out of the blue, a man hits the side of the truck, making me jump.

"Move forward, please!" he shouts. Eliot starts the truck again and I can feel my stomach sink.

The memory of the last time I was here keeps pushing into my mind. Shey's hands shaking, the sickening sound of the slap they gave Ruth. I dig my nails into my palms, try to take my mind somewhere else.

"Paperwork, please."

Eliot reaches for the bundle of papers, passes it over to the soldier. He's not shaved, his skin is red as if he's too hot. He looks at it impatiently, riffles through it. He disappears with it and makes us wait. We watch as he walks across to the booth opposite at the border barrier and disappears inside. I can feel Zuri tense up beside me.

"It's okay," I whisper. "It'll be okay."

I feel her squeeze my fingers. We wait what must be another ten minutes before he returns. "Follow me, please." It's a statement, not a question.

I feel almost numb, they're the same words I heard last time. "We haven't got time for this," says Eliot, trying to stall.

The soldier looks at him. "I don't care," he says. "Come with me now, all of you."

Eliot knows he'll have to get out, walk as if he's not in pain, follow the soldier. He pushes the door open, and I know how much it will hurt him, but I can't help him. The soldier opens the back door for Zuri, and she gets out, doesn't look at him.

He begins to walk away, and Eliot follows him across to the booth, past a few soldiers, their eyes running everywhere, looking for any weakness.

I thought about it afterward, the way that last time they had made Ruth, Shey, and me wait. I'm sure they did it on purpose, so that any uncertainty would bubble to the surface. My stomach is tight, I feel sick. We follow Eliot to where a soldier is looking at some paperwork at a desk in a small wooden shack. He looks up, irritated, and Eliot hangs back, waits for him to say something.

"These your forms?" he asks. "Yes, sir," Eliot replies.

The soldier looks through them again casually, then looks up at Eliot once again. "Haven't seen you before?" he says.

"I'm usually stationed at camp," Eliot replies coolly. He looks back down at the paperwork again.

"And they're married? These three?"

"That's right, sir."

He looks past Eliot now, takes us in. I don't know where to look.

"We've got a long journey ahead," ventures Eliot, hoping it might hurry him a little, but once he's said it, I sense it's a mistake. That any impatience will be punished with even more slowness. The soldier smirks. It's hot, so hot, and some of the other vehicles, ones that were behind us in the queue are being let through. My heart is racing.

"I'm afraid I don't have the authority," he says after a while. "You have to get two signatures on something like this," he says, and my stomach clenches.

"Is that possible?"

The soldier just eyes him neutrally. "Wait here."

Eliot doesn't react as the soldier gets up and wanders out the doorway at the back of the booth. We can't talk, we have to wait. Eliot looks pale and I can see from the way he's shifting his weight that he's slightly unsteady. Eventually we hear two pairs of feet come back. The first guard comes in, picks up the paperwork, and there's someone behind him. I look up, and the figure takes my breath away.

"This is the paperwork," the first soldier says, and picks up the forms, and it takes everything I have not to react as he hands them to Shey.

Shey takes the forms and looks up and our eyes meet, and I feel everything at once. Love, surprise, joy, horror, relief, comfort, everything. And everything is in his eyes too. He tears his eyes away from mine and glances back down at the forms, flicks through them with his fingers, and I can see that he's a man. He's taller, his shoulders are wide, and he has this look, this look of practiced nonchalance that I've seen on soldiers over and over. I search, I desperately want to talk to my Shey, MY Shey, want to find the softness I knew, that I know is still there, somewhere. But I know he can't show me anything, and he just throws down the paperwork on the desk again.

He looks up at us. "You happy to go with this man?" he asks, not looking at me any more than he looks at Zuri or Emily.

We nod.

"Then I don't see what the problem is," he says, looking at the first soldier and picking up a pen. He scribbles a signature on the forms, hands the paperwork to Eliot.

"Have a good journey," he says, and then his voice wavers and he looks over at me. "Be careful out there." I try not to let the tears spring to my eyes. Eliot nods, turns, pulls at my arm because I'm still standing there and not moving back toward the truck.

"This way," he says, to get my attention, and I can't think as he walks me to the truck and opens the door for me. I take my seat, and as Eliot starts the engine, I look across at Shey, who's alone in the booth now, his eyes darkening with tears as he finds mine. I nod at him, and he nods back as the barrier lifts in front of us, revealing the vastness beyond, and suddenly I can feel my heart soar.

Author's Note

It has been predicted that if honeybees were to become extinct, then humans would only have four years to live. The reality seems less dramatic but also more frightening than that. The end of bees would not be an extinction-level event for humans; rather, it would lead to a slow demise and a drastic deterioration in quality of life. There are a hundred crop species that provide 90 percent of food around the world, and seventy-one of these are pollinated by bees.

If honeybees become extinct, the world will be plunged into famine, instability, war, and species collapse. All the plants that bees pollinate will be lost, all the animals that depend on those plants will disappear in a domino effect, and wildlife ecosystems will struggle. This, hand in hand with climate change, could tip the balance of the world, making scientific and medicinal innovation impossible.

Hand pollination is already practiced in some areas of the world, particularly in the Sichuan orchards, as an estimated 80 percent of China's native wild honeybee population has been lost.

I have wanted to write this book for years, but recently it started humming a little louder in my mind. As a beekeeper, I am acutely aware of the interconnectedness of everything and have witnessed firsthand how much the bees are struggling. For many years now, they have been surviving rather than thriving, and as the canary in the coal mine, they are trying to tell us that the state of the natural world is precarious.

I wrote this book in protest against those in power's shortsightedness and our own ambivalence and complacency. I wrote it for my daughter, who will turn thirteen this summer and spends her days painting things. Sometimes I watch her take in every little detail of a moth or a feather and I sense her connectedness to the landscape around her and I think about the fragility of the ecosystem and her future in it. She is brushing up against womanhood in so many ways, and the natural things she marvels at are as vulnerable as her place in the world; after all, the collapse of nature would force us back into gender roles, would give the state even more of an interest in women and girls' reproductive rights and would create a life in which individuality and the arts would be seen as disruptive.

Humanity's greatest weapon with which to tackle the climate emergency is the imagination; we have to make space for creative thinking, and we have to act if we are to succeed. The arts are a powerful way to communicate the urgency of the situation while leading with kindness and compassion. *The Danger of Small Things* is both a love letter to the beauty of nature and a rallying cry; it is a celebration of community and a declaration of my faith that the imagination will ultimately triumph.